emma's STORY

emma's
STORY

from orphan to treasured daughter

BOB SJOGREN and
STEPHANI R. JENKINS

Authentic

COLORADO SPRINGS · MILTON KEYNES · HYDERABAD

Authentic Publishing
We welcome your questions and comments.

USA   1820 Jet Stream Drive, Colorado Springs, CO 80921
        www.authenticbooks.com
UK   9 Holdom Avenue, Bletchley, Milton Keynes, Bucks, MK1 1QR
        www.authenticmedia.co.uk
India   Logos Bhavan, Medchal Road, Jeedimetla Village, Secunderabad
        500 055, A.P.

Emma's Story
ISBN-13: 978-1-934068-40-3
ISBN-10: 1-934068-40-3

Copyright © 2007 by Bob Sjogren and Stephani R. Jenkins

10 09 08 / 6 5 4 3 2 1

Published in 2008 by Authentic
A catalog record for this book is available through the Library of Congress.

Cover and Interior design: projectluz.com
Editorial team: Diane Stortz, Betsy Weinrich, KJ Larson

Printed in the United States of America

This is a fictionalized account of a true story that took place over ten years in a city in Turkey and in Phoenix and Chandler, Arizona. Many of the names of the characters in the book have been changed.

The battle for Emma was a spiritual battle, and we have tried to imagine and communicate events that were taking place in heaven and in the spiritual realm as well as on earth as the battle raged.

May this book give you a vision of God's sovereignty over all events and people, and an understanding of his love for everyone, including those who are handicapped.

—*Bob and Stephani*

Chapter 1

When God called his angels, the heavens echoed with his voice, a sound of indescribable power and tenderness, strength and passion that summoned the angels immediately. There they stood before him, glorious and shining, yet the tallest and brightest among them would never compare to the Lord or to the Son at his right hand. And when God smiled at their swift response to his call, a visible shiver ran through the crowd of celestials standing before his throne. They knew that a meeting like this meant a new revelation of his glory.

"I am beginning a story," God declared, "that will cross the oceans and reveal my glory in ways never seen before. It is a story that will bring hardened hearts into the knowledge of my love. A story to open my light in a darkened land for the very first time."

There was a rustle of robes as a ripple of excitement ran though the angels. Hardened hearts? Darkened land?

"In a certain country, there is an orphanage that houses mentally and physically handicapped children," the Lord continued. "I have claimed these children, who are considered curses by those around them, to be mine. You, my messengers, will help me connect the nations and bring people to these children who will teach them of my love. I will visit some of them personally and work through every circumstance to bring this story about. I will tell you what to do, and my Spirit will be with you."

His gaze met that of one of the angels. "Grace?"

The angel's eyes blazed like fire. "Yes, Lord?"

"Go and encourage Tara, because she will be met with great opposition. My enemy seeks to hide my glory."

"Yes, Lord."

God's face grew soft and tender as he watched Grace disappear to carry out his will. "Let the story begin," He said.

⁂

The shadowy hallway greeted Tara Nelson like the memory of a nightmare. Fluorescent bulbs flickered watery light onto the gray floor, walls, and ceiling and sent eerie shadows dancing down the passages around her. Tara gasped softly as a rat sniffed its way across the floor and disappeared into a hole at the bottom of the flaking plaster wall. She looked back at the hallway behind her. Cobwebs and years of dust hung from the ceiling.

It wasn't too late for her to turn around.

Grace arrived at her side and whispered, "Don't be afraid. Remember why you are here."

Tara looked forward again. She couldn't let fear stop her from doing what she knew she needed to do. She had to think of the children. Where were they, anyway? The children were the reason she had come, and the rooms beyond the hallway should have been full of childish clamor, but Tara could hear nothing. Even the echoes of her footsteps seemed eerily muffled. The woman leading her didn't make any sound either, and her stringy hair and slumped shoulders made Tara sense her despair and hopelessness acutely, as if she had broken the eerie silence with a scream.

⁂

"You called for me, my master?" The demon's voice gurgled and wheezed into the darkness; he hoped he wasn't late.

Two fiery slits appeared above a smoldering smudge in the dark. The master waited and gazed about questioningly. "Report. What of the orphans?" came the impatient reply at last.

"Everything goes well in my sector, my lord," the demon replied, trying to sound confident. "The people are devoted to their religion, and it tells them that those children you asked about are curses. They accept that idea blindly, just as you want them to. Our enemy gets no glory from them."

"Heeehhhhh . . ." A thoughtful wheeze came from his master's voice. "Something will happen with those cursed children soon. My enemy is moving among them; we have seen his messengers lurking about the orphanage. There must be a human who wants to get in to show his love." He wheezed again. "They must not succeed."

"I will send someone immediately, evil one."

"All right, then; get on your way quickly, my demon."

"Yes, my lord."

The burning eyes of the evil one disappeared, leaving the darkness unbroken.

Gaping holes in the walls seemed to scream with despair as Tara passed. In a corner of the ceiling, a spider scurried across its large web. It seemed to be the only other living thing in the building besides Tara and the woman leading her. *Well, maybe I shouldn't count her,* Tara thought, remembering the woman's face—yellow, wrinkled, cold, expressionless.

How many times had her work taken her down nightmarish hallways of one kind or another? So often the work ended in slammed doors, especially here in Turkey. Maybe this time a door would open.

The woman in front of her stopped suddenly at a door. Its polished wood shone brightly in the glow of the single light bulb, a sharp contrast to the rest of the pasty gray building. At eye level, nailed neatly into the oak finish, was a gold rectangle engraved with the words *Head of Orphanage*.

"This is Mr. Kavur's office, Mrs. Nelson," the woman said, speaking in Turkish. "He has been alerted of your presence, so you may go in now."

"Thank you very much," Tara answered.

Tara had prepared what she was going to say to Mr. Kavur a long time ago. Nevertheless, she knew very well that even the most carefully recited speeches could go wrong. *God, please give me strength,* she silently prayed. *I know you want to do something here; I sense your call even as I walk down these halls. And I know that everything will work out the way you want it. This is for you.*

Chapter 2

He wasn't as intimidating as everyone had made him out be, Tara decided. He actually looked kind of jolly. The small round man in front of her sat behind a large oak desk shrouded with paper and looked up at her wearily when she entered the room. Thick grayish-black curls stood out from his head, and he wore a little pair of glasses on the end of a nose that looked like a jellyroll. Just above the rim of the glasses, Tara saw gray eyes that almost matched the color of the long hallway she had just walked.

Grace saw the twisted form of the demon called Pride bending over the man, and the two immortals glared at each other.

"What can I do for you, Mrs. . . . Mrs. . . . ." the man began, also speaking in Turkish.

"Mrs. Nelson," Tara said kindly.

"Nelson, but of course," he finished, nodding to her. "How may I help you?"

Oh, Lord, give me the words, Tara prayed, and then she began, saying, "I am here, Mr. Kavur, at your great establishment, to beg a favor of you. I was wondering, sir, if you would be willing to allow me and a few of my friends to come into your orphanage several hours a week to volunteer. Of course, we know that your workers are already quite capable of giving many comforts to these children that they would not receive otherwise, but my friends and I would like to join your noble work. We could help feed, bathe, and clothe the children, and we can put on special programs with games and treats . . ."

"What a preposterous woman," Pride whispered into Mr. Kavur's ear, "telling you how to run this orphanage. And you know who she is, don't you? Tara Nelson. She and her husband are infidels. They will carry the Christian faith to the ears of the children. You cannot let that happen; Allah forbids it."

Mr. Kavur listened with his hands clasped until Tara had finished speaking. "Mrs. Nelson, although what you offer us here at this orphanage is most gracious, it is impossible. I am sorry." He unclasped his hands and spun his chair around to a filing cabinet at his left, opened one of the drawers, and started to examine the files there.

Tara stood, surprised at how quickly he had rejected her idea. Did this mean that the interview was over? Should she go home now? Maybe he had something else to say. However, as she waited, Mr. Kavur remained silent, reading a paper he had pulled out from a folder in the filing cabinet.

"Try again," Grace said, looking sideways at the smirking demon. The angel knew that the Almighty had more planned than a quick rejection.

"Pardon me," Tara said.

Mr. Kavur looked up. "May I be of further service?" he asked, the creases in his face folding into a strained smile.

"If you do not mind me asking," Tara said slowly, but pleasantly, "why is it impossible for you to allow this?"

"It is impossible, Mrs. Nelson, because I have heard of you and your husband." He also spoke slowly but still in a polite tone of voice. "You are people of the Christian religion, and in this country we are Muslim. The children in this orphanage are raised in that faith, and"—he spoke each word emphatically, as if explaining to one of the children—"I will not allow you or your friends to influence them in the Christian faith. That is all, Mrs. Nelson. Good day." He turned back to the filing cabinet.

"I understand, sir, and I will respect your wishes. Thank you for your time, and have a good day."

The demon chuckled. "Too bad."

At home in Chandler, Arizona, Becky Bates shifted a little in her patio chair. The breeze whispering in the trees was like God's breath playing across her face, rhythmic and comforting in the toasty morning.

It had been four years since Becky had traveled to Turkey with her husband, Graham. Their hearts had been moved, pulling them toward the people they saw and met and worked with. The children especially had touched them, small faces peering at them on street corners and staring out from cracked windows curtained with what looked like dirty dish towels. Those large dark eyes cried out to both of them, asking them—or anyone—to care.

Four years since that trip, yet the tug on their hearts was still strong! Becky and Graham had prayed and waited, prayed and waited, and waited. And waited. *God,* Becky prayed silently, *there's something coming.* She fingered the silky pages of her Bible. *Sometimes it's hard to be patient, waiting for whatever it is you have planned. Please continue to keep me patient. It seems like we've spent the last few years in limbo, and now that Graham's started the insurance business again. . . . Lord, I just give this to you. May you be glorified in whatever we do.*

It was hard for Becky to stay rooted at home while the memory of those precious eyes haunted her. Their home had been empty of children for a long time now. Amy, the oldest, was married and had three children of her own. Becky and Graham's other three children, Adam, Aaron, and Abby—all adopted from Korea—were starting careers and launching their own lives.

Although she loved being a grandmother and volunteering at Frontiers, the missions agency in Phoenix, Becky continued to feel pulled toward the eyes of the children she had seen in Turkey. Graham always told her to be patient and that they would simply have to keep praying; he felt the same pull she did. Becky flipped through the pages of her Bible and read in Matthew, "The King will reply, 'I tell you the truth, whatever you did for one of the least of these brothers of mine, you did for me.'"

Wow, God, that was a faster rejection than I was expecting, Tara thought wryly. She had expected her request to be rejected at her first meeting with Mr. Kavur. More than twenty years of working as a missionary in this Muslim country had prepared her for that. But being dismissed so quickly had surprised her.

"You should just give up," Pride whispered.
"But you won't," said Grace.
The two immortals glared at each other.

"Well, I'll just have to try again next week," Tara said out loud.

Grace smiled, and the demon growled with anger.

Chapter 3

Christians in Turkey were used to being denied requests because of their faith. But God had always been faithful, Tara reminded herself. All she needed to do was not give up. The following week she found herself again in front of the polished oak door, praying one last time before she asked the same question as the week before.

She got the same answer. "That is still most gracious of you, Mrs. Nelson. But it is impossible."

Grace whispered, "Don't give up, Tara. Your heavenly Father has a plan. What door he opens, no man can shut."

Tara somehow felt encouraged as she drove back down the narrow, crowded streets toward home. She resolved to try again the next week.

"I know God is calling me to do something in there, Ben," she explained to her husband that night. "If you could just see those kids for a moment, you'd realize how much we are needed."

"You ARE needed. Jesus is needed," said Grace, still by Tara's side.

"Just keep plugging along, honey," Ben responded. "If God wants it, He'll do it."

"Hope," the Lord summoned his angel softly.

Hope appeared at his feet. "You called me, Lord?"

"What do you think of my precious child, My Bahar, and about what has happened since I charged you with her care?"

Hope gazed into the light from the Lord's face, squinting slightly. "Her life has just begun," he answered, "and already it is full of trials, as you said it would be. But I comfort her."

Sadness for the pain Bahar was in crossed the Lord's face. He had marked Bahar for a special purpose, and in order for that purpose to be carried out, she had to go through these trials. "Well, done, Hope," He said. "Be encouraged, because her story will soon change. Now—"

Suddenly the Lord's gaze shifted beyond Hope. "Come away from the shadows, dark one."

Hope whirled around. His eyes grew wide, and he whipped out his sword and held it ready, the blade flickering like tongues of flame.

"Heeehhhh. Tell your angel to drop his sword. He has no need of it right now."

The voice that came from the shrouded figure in front of them slid through the light and seemed to drag Hope's thoughts into darkness. Hope shook his head and grasped his sword more firmly.

"I said put that sword down, angel. You don't need it. I wouldn't try to strike you in his presence." Satan lifted his hooded head from his crouching form.

Hope could see two eyes like burning coals shining inside the hood. The next moment Hope's sword turned cold, so cold that his hands began to sting and the light from his fingers dimmed. He gasped for breath, fighting to keep hold of his icy weapon.

"Stop your games, Satan," boomed the Lord's voice, and the rays shining from his face burned brighter.

Hope's sword grew warm again.

"Put away your sword, Hope."

Hope obeyed.

"Do not harass my angels before me," the Lord growled as his gaze turned to Satan.

Satan's demeanor shrank.

"You have come for answers," the Lord and King said.

"Perhaps," Satan rasped, shielding his face with a scaly, skeletal hand. The light from the Almighty shimmered upon him nevertheless. "I have come to see what goes on in this place."

"Have you seen my daughter, Tara, and the work she has done?" the Lord asked, smiling slightly. He already knew the answer to his question.

"What work?" Satan hissed. "She has done nothing except waste her time. And what of this Bahar you spoke of?"

"She has a part in Tara's undertaking, and so do Becky and Graham."

"Becky and Graham? They are halfway across the world."

"That's not too far for me," the Lord answered. "Their hearts are obedient, and they will receive my call. They, Tara, and Bahar will all be united and will reveal my name, not only to the children you try so hard to keep from me but also to many other nations. Many people will hear this story and see my glory."

Satan rose up indignantly, pulled his hand away from his face, and spat. "If you do this," he wheezed, "I will fight you every step of the way. Those children and those people are too far in my clutches for me to let them go now. Heh, heeehhhh." He paced back and forth and then pointed a long, twisted finger at the Lord. "They may follow your call, but they will pay for it! Whatever you do, I will turn to evil! Whoever you send, I will meet with trials! Wherever you go, I will stop you!"

Hope watched as God leaned down until he finally met Satan eye to eye. He smiled as the fallen angel, eyes smoldering with pain and anger, tried to remain standing erect. God's face, however, was calm, and

Hope shivered in awe as he spoke in a low voice that seemed to rumble throughout the very foundations of heaven.

"Just try to stop me."

Chapter 4

Nimet bent low over the crib and gazed at the face of her daughter. In the baby's eyes Nimet found an anchor, a clear image in a world fogged and hazy to her senses. Most of the time, her mind was so hazy she couldn't even remember that she had a daughter.

Tucking a piece of her long dark hair behind her ear, she carefully lifted her baby into her arms. She cradled her, rocking her back and forth, singing the blessing of Allah that Nimet's mother had sung to her and that her grandmother had sung before then. Right now Nimet could almost fight the urge to take more of her medicine. She felt strong with her daughter in her arms.

But the baby began to cry. Suddenly Nimet's strength drained. She laid the baby on the bed and changed her. She offered her breast, but the baby refused it. She tried rocking again, back and forth, but the baby still wailed. Nimet began to flounder. *Why did I even pick her up? Why did I disturb her?*

Bahar's wails grew louder.

"You thought you could handle her, didn't you?" the demon Despair whispered. *"But you can't, can you? You're a terrible mother. You can't even calm her down. What an embarrassment you are to your husband."*

Nimet fought tears and placed her daughter back in her crib. She felt even more sick and dizzy.

"You need your medicine," whispered Despair.

Where was her medicine? She left the bedroom and scrambled around the house until she found it. She would feel calm again once she took her pills.

But the pills would not stop the baby's screaming, so Nimet shut the door of the bedroom and distracted herself in the kitchen. *Too many pills, too often,* she thought. She didn't want to have to tell Sakir that he would need to obtain more pills for her soon.

Sakir didn't like the screaming either.

"What is wrong with you, woman? Why can you not get that child to be silent when I am around?" he growled angrily that evening as Bahar continued to scream.

"You see, you're not only a terrible mother, you're a terrible wife," *Despair hinted.*

"My head hurts, and I feel dizzy," Nimet objected.

"Your head hurts every time something goes wrong," her husband muttered. "Can't you do something better than take medicine all the time?"

He thrust the newspaper down and turned toward the bedroom door. The walls seemed to be vibrating with the baby's crying.

"It's so loud . . ." *Despair whined in Sakir's ear.*

"Do something about that noise!" Sakir screamed. "By Allah, she is only an infant!"

Hope watched sorrowfully, even though he knew the Lord had a

emma's STORY

purpose for the pain in this household.

"*There is nothing you can do, woman,*" said Despair. "*You are too sick to handle anything so strenuous . . .*"

Nimet heaved herself from her chair. "I am useless with that child, husband. Besides, it gets harder and harder to move these days. I don't know how long this body will last. Allah makes my days cursed."

Disgusted, Sakir stormed out of the house. He tried to push thoughts of his wife and daughter to the back of his mind. He did not like to think of them.

"*It's impossible for you to raise that child with your income and an incompetent wife,*" whispered Despair. His eyes glowed at the worry that creased Sakir's forehead.

Sakir shook his head quickly, as if trying to dislodge the thoughts. What was the baby's name again, anyway? *Oh, yes, Bahar.*

Walking down the gray halls for the third time, Tara prayed, *Lord, could this be the day that Mr. Kavur says yes?* She dared to think it could.

"*You're fooling yourself,*" Deceit whispered. "*He's not going to see you again; this is a waste of time. Why not just leave?*"

Tara heard Mr. Kavur sigh when she entered his office.

"You again?" It was a question and a statement at the same time. *At least he recognizes me.* "Yes, I've come to ask if you would give us the honor of blessing the children and allowing us to feed and love them."

"I'm so sorry, but that is impossible. You're wasting your time, Mrs. Nelson. Good day."

He's getting faster at dismissing me, she thought. But that was all right; she would be back again in a week.

Before she drove away, Tara turned to look again at the orphanage and the rusty chain-link fence that marked its boundaries.

George Carey was enjoying getting to know all the families in the church he was now pastoring. Becky and Graham Bates told a story that completely fascinated him.

"So," he said to Becky and Graham, "God has given you a heart for these Muslim children. How in the world did that happen?"

Graham ran a hand over his short, graying curls. "Four years ago. We went over with Bob Sjogren while we were both volunteering with Frontiers. It was our first time in a Muslim country, and God really did a work in our hearts."

"Especially concerning the children," Becky added. "So many of them were homeless and dirt poor. I just wanted to take every one of them home with me and love them."

Graham nodded. "And, basically, we've never been able to get the kids of Turkey out of our hearts."

"And you still want to do something to help them?" Pastor George asked.

"That's right," said Becky, "but none of our contacts has been able to help us. Every time we look into something, God just seems to shut the door."

emma's STORY

Chapter 5

One Year Later

The yellow-skinned, gray-haired woman looked up and smiled as Tara entered the orphanage. "Good afternoon, Mrs. Nelson."

"Good afternoon, Marif," said Tara. She had developed relationships with some of the orphanage workers. "How did your son's soccer game go?"

"Very well." Marif's smile grew wider. "He scored two goals and was awarded Most Valuable Player by his coach. He's decided that he wants to play professional soccer. Mr. Kavur told me to tell you that he will be in a meeting until four o'clock."

Tara glanced up at the clock above the desk. The glass and both hands were missing.

"Oh, you have about fifteen minutes," Marif said quickly. "I'm sorry, that clock broke this week."

Tara nodded. She moved to the other side of the room and sat on a wooden chair against the gray wall.

"Why are you here?" Doubt hissed. "What good are you doing, wasting your time every week simply to be a nuisance? You've wasted an entire year. There are other places that need you more. You should focus on them."

Why was she here? The orphanage was nearly an hour from her house. Week after week, month after month, the drive seemed to grow longer each time. Why was she bothering? Then again, Tara was being rejected so quickly now that it was *only* the drive that took much time.

"It's such a bother," Doubt continued.

Suddenly, another demon appeared beside Doubt and whispered into his ear. Doubt felt his eyes bulge. Waving the demon away, Doubt turned quickly and hunched over Tara. "Yes, why bother coming here? You should just go home. . . . Don't even wait for Mr. Kavur to see you. Stop being a nuisance here and return to where you can do some real good."

Tara wondered if she should bother Mr. Kavur by coming into his office right after the meeting he was currently having.

Something sharp suddenly jabbed Doubt's shoulder, demanding his attention. Turning, he met Grace's stony face. The angel's sword was drawn, and his light was flaring powerfully.

"Leave here, demon. You cannot stop the Lord's work."

Doubt's eyes narrowed, their smoldering light twisting with evil. "She is already poisoned, angel. My master's grip in here is too strong for any plan of your lord. I'm not leaving."

"Let's find out," Grace said in a low, challenging voice. He swung his sword.

Doubt ducked and rolled out of reach, then leaped back to his feet and drew his own weapon. The blade seemed to squirm around Grace's hand and suck away the light around it. The demon cackled wildly and leaped forward to attack. Grace blocked his downward thrust.

The heavenly light around Grace stung Doubt's eyes and forced him to stumble and look away, but only for a moment. When he turned back, his eyes were filled with an angry, writhing glow, and with it he tried to suck away the angel's light.

He attacked a second time. Grace was ready to block, but the demon's sword seemed to twist around Grace's own weapon, and the dark blade pierced Grace's shoulder. Grace cut upward with his sword and caught the demon between the ribs. The heavenly blade seemed to melt the demon away, and with a howl of anger he disappeared.

Go on, thought Grace. Slink back to your master. He's sure to punish you for losing the battle. "Holy is the Lord God Almighty," he said aloud. He looked at his shoulder. The wound was already closed up, and his robe was mended.

Turning back to where Doubt had disappeared, Grace nodded sadly. Once they both had been a part of the heavenly host. But some of the angels had chosen to follow Satan, and now the immortals would wrestle against each other until God ended the war.

"Grace, remember your mission," the Spirit of the Lord gently reminded.

"Mrs. Nelson?" said Marif. "Mr. Kavur should be finished with his board meeting any moment."

As four o'clock came, Tara was ushered into Ezhan Kavur's office. Mr. Kavur gestured toward the chair in front of his desk. *That's strange,* Tara thought. *He stopped gesturing for me to sit down months ago.*

Mr. Kavur adjusted his glasses on the end of his nose, then clasped his hands. "Now, Mrs. Nelson, I assume you have come for the same reason . . . to ask permission to help the children?"

"Yes, that's right."

"Of course. And I assume you know that I have just had a meeting with the orphanage board?"

"I just found out."

"All right. But I assume you hope that perhaps something has occurred from that meeting that will help you and your little proposal. Am I right?"

"Actually, sir, I hadn't considered that."

"Oh?" Mr. Kavur's forehead wrinkled. "Well, nevertheless," he continued, his brow smoothing out and a pleasant expression lighting his features, "your request was mentioned to the board this afternoon, and we have come to a conclusion that will end our little weekly meetings."

Tara sat still as a stone. They were going to prevent her from asking anymore.

Grace smiled as he watched.

"Mrs. Nelson, you have been coming to me with the same request for over a year. Every week you come in here. So, when I spoke to the board about you, we decided that we admire your persistence and are willing to grant your request."

Tara blinked.

"Well done, My child," the Lord said, and the angels watching the scene erupted in applause.

"It's true, Tara. It is true," Grace said. "The door has opened, and the harvest is ripe."

"I . . . I . . . Many thanks, Mr. Kavur. I am truly grateful."

Mr. Kavur smiled pleasantly again. "There *are* just a few conditions, Mrs. Nelson." He unclasped his hands. "And one of them is this: we cannot allow you to come into contact with our normal children, because of the influence your faith may have on them. However . . ." He picked up a small stack of papers lying on his desk. "We have a section in the orphanage for handicapped children. I can allow you and your people to work with them. Of course, many of the children are so retarded that there is not much you can do to help them. Our workers do almost everything possible."

Mr. Kavur handed the papers to Tara. "Here are the rules and a map of the orphanage. We expect you and any others you bring here to follow those rules faithfully and to get permission from us before doing anything." He resettled his glasses on his nose. "I really don't know how much you can do for handicapped children, but I suppose this is something, isn't it? Good day, Mrs. Nelson."

Chapter 6

For the moment, the small house was quiet. Sakir sat beside the kitchen table, holding a newspaper open in front of him, though he'd barely glanced at it. Sakir's mind was elsewhere, and his jaw was tightly clenched. He always felt tension when he thought of his family. Although it wasn't that he actually tried to think of them; the thoughts just seemed to rush upon him unbidden, pressing in, whispers that grew louder and louder. Today the whispers were especially cruel. But they had reason to be.

"How will you tell Nimet?" Despair whispered.

Sakir dropped the newspaper onto the table and rubbed his forehead. He had worked so hard, for so long, and now this! Even though he had been home for hours, what had happened today still didn't seem real. What should he do next? How would he pay for Bahar to grow up? How could he get his wife more medicine to keep her calm? Why did this have to happen?

"Why?" the demon hissed. "Allah must be displeased with you. Why else would he let you lose your job like this?"

Sakir couldn't see any other reason for these burdens, and yet he couldn't understand how he had displeased Allah. He had always been devoted to Islam. He prayed diligently all of his life, just like any good Muslim, and he fasted from sunrise to sunset every day during the month of Ramadan. When he was a young man, he had even made a pilgrimage to the holy city of Mecca to remember Muhammed, Allah's greatest prophet.

Sakir longed for those golden days when he and Nimet were younger and the world had held so much promise. But years had passed, and something had changed. He should not have allowed Nimet to get addicted to the medicine she took for her depression. And when Bahar came, it only got worse. Deep down, he loved them, but there was a struggle inside him that he felt he could not win.

Allah's ways are not for man to understand. Maybe he should go tell Nimet about his job and just get it over with. Pushing back his chair, Sakir got up from the table and walked into the bedroom.

C:)

After the Sunday service, Pastor George noticed Graham and Becky moving down the aisle toward the door.

"Go tell them about next week," Unity urged him. *The Lord didn't want Graham and Becky to miss what he was sending them.*

Pastor George made his way toward the door, hoping to catch Graham and Becky. He had forgotten to tell them about next week's guest speaker, Alan Grant. Alan might be the answer to their prayers.

"George, you're just the person I wanted to see."

George turned around. "Josh, good to see you," he said as they shook hands.

"You too. Hey, I was wondering if you had a minute to meet my father?"

Over his shoulder, George saw Graham and Becky go out to the parking lot. *Too bad,* he thought. He would have to try to call them sometime during the week.

Unity spotted an older man a few feet from Josh's father. He positioned himself at the man's side and whispered, "There's a visitor here who needs someone to speak to him," and then he smiled as the man walked over to Josh's father and introduced himself.

Josh saw that his father was already engaged in conversation. "Well, it looks like he's busy," he said to Pastor George. "Is it all right if I introduce you a little later?"

"Not a problem. There's a couple I wanted to speak to before they left, anyway."

"All right, then." Josh nodded to George and moved to join his father.

Unity smiled and nudged the pastor. "Go quickly!" he urged.

George hurried down the aisle and out the door. "Graham! Becky!" He spotted them just climbing into their car and ran to catch them. "Good morning! Hey, you two weren't heading up to the mountains next week, were you?"

"Well, we were planning on it, George," Graham said. "With this summer heat, I thought we'd get a breath of cool air. Why?"

"You know we've got a special speaker coming next Sunday, and I was talking to him a few evenings ago—discussing what he was going to talk about during the sermon and such—and he works with some missionaries in Turkey. They just got permission for Americans to come and minister in an orphanage near where they live. Can you believe it? A Muslim country and they've said yes! And since you want to go back to Turkey, I thought you two would be interested."

Graham and Becky exchanged looks, and Becky could hardly conceal the hope bubbling up inside her.

Unity smiled too. "Well done," he heard the Lord say.

⁂

As Becky and Graham listened to Alan Grant speak of Tara's story, Becky felt that their own story seemed to open up before them. Her mind buzzed with questions. Was Tara the answer to all of their prayers? Could they go and visit and talk with Tara? Could they be a part of the work at the orphanage?

After the service, Alan Grant put them in touch with Tara, and four weeks later, Graham and Becky and Pastor George flew to Turkey to visit the orphanage.

⁂

Deep within the dark of his own fallen kingdom, Satan listened as his demons told him of seeing three of the enemy's children crossing the Atlantic Ocean. Fools! They would undoubtedly try to loosen his hold in the orphanage. His eyes glowed with anger, and his mouth pressed into a hard line.

"Confusion," he hissed.

A demon appeared at his clawed feet. "You summoned me, my master?"

"I have work for you."

Chapter 7

*C*onfusion and Doubt watched Graham and Becky and their pastor *in the airport. Grinning maliciously, the two demons moved past the trio and into baggage claim.*

"Do either of you see those duffel bags we brought for the kids?" George asked.

"Nope," Graham and Becky answered together. Six pieces of luggage were missing, the ones with the small toys, candy, shoes, and clothes.

Confusion and Doubt laughed.

Graham reached up and rubbed the back of his neck, thinking. "Well," he said, "let's go ask someone." He and George loaded the bags that had arrived onto two carts, and Becky followed as they made their way toward a blue-uniformed airport employee. The man didn't speak English, so Becky improvised with hand motions and sound effects to try to communicate their problem. He motioned for them to follow him to another part of the airport, where they saw a doorway with a long line of people standing in front of it.

Confusion rubbed his claws together in anticipation.

"Let me guess," Becky whispered to Graham. "Our bags are somewhere here, in customs."

emma's STORY

Tara shifted from foot to foot, watching as the faces in the airport pushed by her. Her hands were getting tired of holding the piece of paper in front of her. There was still no sign of the people whose names were printed across the paper—Graham & Becky Bates, George Carey. Maybe she should double-check that their flight had come in. But she'd already done that. She looked at her watch again.

Lord, only you know where Graham, Becky, and George are right now. Ever since she first talked to Becky on the phone, Tara had felt as if she were walking on clouds. Only God could have brought the Bateses to her at this particular time. The past few weeks at the orphanage had gone well, but Tara was beginning to realize how big the project she had undertaken really was. She and her friends could only do so much for the children in two days a week, two hours each day. It took almost all of that time to simply hug forty children who were in one room.

Tara checked her watch again. It was almost an hour later than she was supposed to meet the trio from America.

"Move around the airport," Grace encouraged her. *"Maybe they're waiting for you somewhere else."*

Okay, that's enough, Tara decided. She headed up the hallway they should have come down. Maybe she could hold up the sign in other areas of the airport in case they had gotten lost. Was she right in leaving? She wasn't sure, but she felt that she had to do something.

Six large duffel bags sat in the middle of the customs room like a small mountain. Apparently, they had drawn some suspicion from officials. One of the customs workers asked, in halting English, "What is the purpose of the toys, candy, and clothing in the bags?"

"We are bringing them for children," George said, slowly and clearly. "To give as gifts."

The worker shook his head. "I am sorry," he said, equally carefully. "My English is not good. Please, again."

Becky smiled and pretended to hand something to a smaller person. "We brought these for children. To . . . give. For . . . children."

The customs workers all shook their heads.

"Tara is expecting you," Doubt whispered. "What will she do when you don't show up?"

"For little ones," Becky explained impatiently, worrying that Tara might leave without them. "For children to get and be happy." She pretended to hold one of the stuffed animals and dance it around in the air.

"Little ones," Graham repeated, gesturing at the height of a small child.

The workers looked at each other, still baffled.

Confusion stood in their midst, looking triumphant.

Lord, this isn't working, Becky prayed. *Please do something.* She turned her head and watched the people rushing past the glass doors. She felt confused, even in despair.

The two demons smiled.

Suddenly, Becky spotted a figure standing just beyond the line of people outside the door, a woman with graying hair holding up a piece of paper with three names on it—their names! "Graham! Look over there!"

George had spotted Tara too and was pointing and pantomiming a request for her to be allowed in. Eventually, one of customs workers brought Tara into the room.

"Tara?" asked Becky.

"Yes! And I'm so glad to meet you. I'd almost given up looking for you!"

"There's a problem with some of our bags," Graham said.

Tara spoke to the customs workers and gestured apologetically to the duffel bags on the floor. Exclamations of understanding and smiles came from the workers, and soon two carts arrived for the duffel bags.

"Well, everything's all right," said Tara, "and they want to help us by pushing the bags wherever we need them to go."

"That's great!" Becky exclaimed. "And from here on, you're in charge. So we'll follow you."

Confusion and Doubt watched Tara and her new friends leave the airport. Everything had been going so well! Confusion shook his head and turned to his comrade. "There weren't even any angels to try to stop us," he growled.

The two demons exchanged looks. They both knew that there was someone stronger than just the angels pulling the Bateses toward the orphanage. And there was nothing they could do to stop him.

"The master will be angry," Doubt said.

Chapter 8

"Great dinner, Tara, thank you," said George, putting down his fork. "Now tell us again, what finally made customs surrender our bags this afternoon?"

Ben looked up. "I didn't hear about a run-in with customs," he protested, though with a smile. "What did you do, honey?"

"Oh, really, not that much. Customs was wondering about the duffels of treats for the kids, so I said they were for Children's Day."

"Yeah, what's that again?" Graham asked.

"It's a national holiday here when people give little presents to the kids."

"That was very clever," Ben said. "Especially since that's essentially what you guys are doing. Those kids have probably never had a Children's Day."

"Would they have let our bags through if the gifts weren't specifically for Children's Day?" Graham wondered aloud.

"Who knows?" Ben answered. "The reality is that they probably weren't even suspicious of your bags. They just saw an opportunity to make some money off rich American tourists."

"At least this way you have a legal holiday to back you up," Tara added.

"So, Tara, what's the plan for tomorrow?" Becky asked.

"Well, if I can pick you three up at your hotel by noon, we'll get to the orphanage by one o'clock." Her eyes twinkled with amusement. "You Americans have got the orphanage in a pretty big stir. Ezhan Kavur wants to meet you and give you a tour of the grounds and everything."

"Does he know why we're here?" Graham asked.

"He knows what you are coming to do," Tara answered slowly, "but as far as *why* you're spending your time and money to visit with handicapped kids, I'm sure he doesn't have the foggiest idea."

Grace smiled. Not even Tara had the foggiest idea of what was going to happen.

⁕

"Why can't you control yourself, woman? I just got that bottle two days ago! Why does Allah curse me with your gluttony?" Sakir cursed at his wife.

"You made me this way, husband!" Nimet snapped back. "When you first came home with that medicine—you should have known it would bind me like this! You told me that you would make me well again. But you only gave me medicine to appease me so I wouldn't be a bother!" Her voice wavered desperately. "Now you have made me sicker than before; and all day I can hardly even rise from my bed."

Bahar had pulled herself up into a sitting position and curled her fingers around the bars of her crib. She heard a crash from the room beyond.

Hope was startled at the noise of the crash and hovered defensively over Bahar's bed.
"I'm here to protect you, little one. No need to fear."

Bahar turned her head toward the wall, but she didn't cry. She never cried when her parents were fighting.

Sakir had started shouting again, his voice rising over Nimet's sobs. "I only tried to make you happy! And now you curse me for it! If you want more of your drug, you must get off the couch and get it. I am finished serving your greed. I spend my life always trying to help us! I need to find a place to work! I need to find a way for us to eat and be clothed. Stop wailing, woman! You wonder why I leave and don't come back for a long time. Your wailing answers that for you!"

Nimet began to moan, holding her stomach and rocking back and forth. "Please, Sakir," she gasped. "I am sorry that I am such a bad person. I don't know why I have felt so much sicker these last few weeks. Please, if you could only bring me some more of my medicine, I will not trouble you again. I will grow stronger; and I will—"

"I've heard your lies many times, woman. Don't bother to go on with them. I told you that I am done. If you want your drugs, you know how to get them. I am leaving to find a job."

Bahar heard the door to the street open.

"You are a wasted man!" Nimet shrieked as the door slammed shut. "There is no job that anyone will ever want you to do!"

For several moments, Bahar heard only the sudden silence that seemed to echo off the walls. Then a loud groan came from the other room, followed by the twang of the couch springs and Nimet's footsteps lumbering across the floor.

Hope watched the door as the sound of the footsteps grew louder.

Bahar cringed when the door was shoved open. Sometimes after her parents argued, her mother had come into the room and started hitting her. Bahar's heart beat wildly.

"Not this time," the angel whispered, placing a hand on Bahar's head.

Bahar buried herself underneath the threadbare blanket in her crib and peered through a hole in the fabric. Her mother lumbered to the dresser and snatched a long black scarf from on top of a pile of clothes.

"I'm going to die," Nimet panted, tying the scarf over her head. "I'm going to die just getting the medicine he should get for me. Allah will judge him for that." Suddenly she moaned and leaned against the end of the bed. "Oh, why do I feel so bad?" she cried.

"Just leave, woman," Hope whispered. He could see Bahar watching her mother through the hole in the blanket, her eyes wide with fear.

That night, Becky sat in front of the window in their hotel room and gazed at the bustling city below them. "We're really here, Graham."

"I know. Tomorrow's going to be interesting. We've heard what Tara said—about what that orphanage is like. What do you think?"

"I have a hard time imagining that any place can be as bad as she says. It sounds so much worse than even the worst of what we saw four years ago. I guess we'll just have to wait and see. The funny thing is, I'm not nervous about this at all."

"That's good," Graham said, concealing his own nervousness. What was this place that could treat kids so badly? How would the people at the orphanage react to their visit? What about the kids themselves? He looked at his wife's silhouette in the lingering glow of the sunset. Silently, he prayed.

Chapter 9

*T*he next afternoon, Grace, Unity, and Strength all flanked the group heading across the pock-marked sidewalk to the orphanage. The angels' swords were drawn and burning vibrantly.

"This place smells like the evil one," said Grace, gripping his sword more tightly.

"Be on your guard," answered Unity.

The hinges creaked and squealed in protest as Tara began to push open the large wooden doors.

"Ready, folks?" she asked.

"Come what may," said Becky, as Graham and George nodded.

Inside, Becky was surprised. She had expected far worse. The ceiling tiles were water stained, and the carpet should have been replaced twenty years ago, but that was the worst of the room. She tried to hide her grin when she saw a clock with no glass and no hands above the reception desk.

Mr. Kavur and some others stepped into the room, bowed, and then shook hands with the Americans. The top of Mr. Kavur's head barely reached Becky's shoulder.

"Welcome to our institution," Tara translated as the little man began to speak. "We're honored by your visit and pray that you have so far found your stay in our country satisfactory."

Becky smiled and nodded. "We've found it very satisfactory, and thank you for opening your doors to us on such short notice."

Mr. Kavur grinned and spoke again, waving his hand at his guests in a pleased way.

"He says that this is a great pleasure and that he always had a good feeling about this new program," Tara translated.

Graham coughed.

The foursome was introduced to the orphanage employees and two members of the orphanage board.

"It is an honor that board members came to meet you," Tara said.

Grace eyed the snarling demons crouched in the corner and beside the desk.

"They're watching us," Unity whispered.

"The Lord said they wouldn't attack us this time," said Strength, "but they do look angry enough to do something foul."

"It's because the Lord is reclaiming his hold here," Unity said, "and they don't like it."

"They don't have a choice, not when his Spirit stops them," said Strength, and he moved to follow the crowd of people down the hallway.

"Tara," George called, holding up the camera around his neck. Tara nodded and asked Mr. Kavur if they could take pictures on their tour. Mr. Kavur shook his head no.

The group continued down the hall. After a brief tour of the offices, the orphanage workers excused themselves from the tour, leaving Mr. Kavur and the two board members with Tara and her guests.

"Now he's going to take us to the handicapped building." Tara said, following the little man out the back door.

The group made its way down a cracked, narrow sidewalk and began passing huge gray buildings. Each building looked like all the others, the only variations being holes and splotches of mildew growing up the sides in different places.

"How much further is the handicapped building?" Becky asked. She was panting.

"We're close now," Tara answered.

More demons peered at the party from around the corners of the buildings, but they never tried to approach.

Finally, Mr. Kavur and the board members stopped in front of—*surprise, surprise,* thought Becky—another big gray building. The door opened and everyone filed inside.

The reception room in this building was much worse than the first. Spiderwebs hung heavily in the corners, and bits of fallen ceiling plaster were scattered across the cracked linoleum floor. One corner of the room had mold creeping up the walls.

A wispy-haired woman jumped up from behind the desk and nodded to the party filing in.

"This is the handicapped building," Tara translated for Mr. Kavur, "with eight rooms full of children."

The wispy-haired woman gave everyone disposable paper slippers to put over their shoes, and then the foursome followed Mr. Kavur down the hallway. As they got deeper into the building, conditions worsened. Becky tried not to gag; she gave up trying to breathe only through her mouth because the stench seemed to sneak into her nose regardless. She wondered if the paper slippers they had on were for their protection and not the orphanage's. The floor was stained a variety of moldy colors, the dirt and dust turning all of them into shades of brownish gray.

Looking up, Becky saw that whole sections of the ceiling had crumbled away, leaving only the insulation showing now. On either side of the hallway were steel doors, shut and, as far as Becky could tell, locked. By each door, a worker sat on a chair. One of the chairs the party passed only had three legs; two cinder blocks were stacked up where the fourth leg should have been.

"Where's all the noise?" Becky whispered to Graham. According to Mr. Kavur, this particular building held about three hundred children, but the halls were deathly quiet, except for soft strains of Middle Eastern music. Becky shivered.

Chapter 10

"He's going to take us to see some of the children now," said Tara. "Prepare yourselves."

The group followed Mr. Kavur into a room with an open steel door.

Becky grabbed Graham's hand. The children that lay before them in the painted metal cribs looked like they had come from a horror movie. All of their hair had been shaved so shampoos would not be necessary; their scrawny bodies screamed of hunger, and their eyes stared blankly at the group that crowded into their cave-like room.

Becky gazed at the faces. She saw cracked and missing teeth, bony wrists and ankles tied with rags to the bars of the cribs, and crossed eyes. Some of the children had cloudy, blinded eyes. An old tape player from somewhere in the back of the room played the slow, haunting music she had heard before.

The angels tensed when the demons in the room stood. One of the angry faces hissed, but the demons all backed away from the group surrounded by the Spirit.

"These are the children," Tara translated. "In this room they range from age ten to twenty-two." She paused as Mr. Kavur continued speaking and motioned to the cribs. "As you will notice, some of them are restrained by scarves tied to the crib. This is because they have exhibited violent behavior, and we do not wish for them to harm themselves or our workers."

There were no cribs in the next room. Instead, a sofa with cushions like empty pillowcases stood at one end of the room. Several children who were sprawled on it sat up when Mr. Kavur entered with Becky and the others. At least thirty other children were sitting or lying on the bare floor. Some struggled for several minutes to squirm around to see the group. The faces of these children looked much the same as those in the previous room. One boy was tied to a radiator with a scarf that went around his waist.

"This is the playroom for the children," Mr. Kavur said through Tara. *Playroom?* thought Becky. *A sagging couch and old linoleum flooring? This is some place to play.* She gazed around at the faces staring up at her. They looked intensely curious, but Becky saw fear as well.

One little child was staring right at Graham; there wasn't any fear behind those eyes, Becky noticed. Graham smiled and knelt down on one knee. The child belonging to the eyes jumped up and ran to him, arms outstretched, and giggled as Graham scooped the little body into his arms. Graham sat down on the couch, and the child—a little girl, Becky decided—giggled some more and put her arms around his neck. It seemed that not all the children here were physically handicapped.

When he saw the pair on the couch, Mr. Kavur said something to Tara, gesturing toward George's camera and then to the couch. George got the hint and clicked a picture of Graham and the little girl while Mr. Kavur smiled broadly. The formal tension in the air seemed to ease.

At Tara's suggestion, lunch was taken at the cafeteria with the nonhandicapped children. Becky thought the adults all looked slightly nauseous as the cooks slopped an oily soup with hairy-looking vegetables into their bowls. They all made a great pretense of eating.

After lunch, Mr. Kavur gave permission for their group to have free reign of the handicapped building. For a while, they simply wandered the halls together, peeking into different rooms and greeting the workers who guarded the steel doors.

Becky walked ahead, praying. *Well, Lord, there's certainly a lot of need here. This place—these kids—need so much that I would be overwhelmed if I didn't already know you're big enough to handle all this. And it is all for your glory anyway.* This place made her want to feel God's presence as much as possible. Becky turned and saw the others meandering far behind her. The door on her right was open, so she stopped and peeked in.

Strength, who had been walking by her side, whispered, "He is an ever present strength and shield."

Becky's heart seemed to stop, and she felt her head buzz. A mass of half-naked, bony creatures lay curled up on the floor in front of her, yellowed bulging eyes gazing blankly. Some squirmed on the blue and white linoleum, some twitched convulsively. Layers of yellowed crust flaked from the faces.

Something howled in the far corner. The buzzing in Becky's head increased. These were children! She turned back down the hallway so she wouldn't scream.

Chapter 11

On the way back to the hotel, Becky told the others about the room and asked Tara about it.

"The most severely handicapped kids are put there during the day," Tara said, maneuvering the van through traffic, "and then put across the hall at night. The room you saw is like their playroom."

"Some playroom," George said.

"They say it's just severely mentally retarded behavior," Tara continued.

"Do you believe that?" asked Becky.

"I don't know yet. They do seem worse off than the other handicapped kids."

That night Becky sat a long time watching the street lamps flicker outside her window. The day had left her numb. *I guess we'll find out more tomorrow.*

She didn't sleep well.

The angels in the holy court shimmered and seemed to sing with the presence of their holy maker. Strength, Grace, and Unity approached the glorious throne.

"Well done, my excellent servants," the Lord greeted them. "Your vigilance was noticed in the ranks of the dark one."

The angels bowed their heads, feeling the thrill of his presence.

"The journey through the orphanage was hard for my children," the Lord continued, "and there is still much work to do." His voice pulsed over the angels in a golden wave. "My Spirit will flow through their

actions and words like a storm that cleanses the air. However, when they return, the evil one will begin to fight back."

The angels remembered the dare that had occurred and exchanged glances.

The Lord lifted his head and called through the ranks of celestials on his left and on his right, "Who will go and defend my children?"

The angels rose like one great light, seeming to multiply in number.

He beamed. "My angels, go to my children and fight the opposition that rises against them. Satan will fall as surely as you fight, because I am with you."

"Okay," Tara said, standing outside the first room Mr. Kavur had shown them the day before. "They said we could start in this room. If we get a good reaction from the kids, we'll move on down the hall." She pushed open the steel door. "Just set it all on the floor."

Graham and George, staggering under the weight of three voluminous duffel bags, did what she asked. Becky looked into the eyes of the children. They gazed blankly as Tara unzipped one of the duffels and rummaged through the toys and bags of candy.

"These kids have experienced so little human touch," Tara said. "They might be a little scared at first, but they'll warm up to us in no time. I hope." She pulled a small stuffed rabbit from the bag and walked up to one of the cribs.

The child in the crib cringed, twisting into a ball and covering his head with large, misshapen hands when she knelt down next to him.

"It's okay," Tara cooed in Turkish. "Peace for you, little one. I'm not going to hurt you."

The boy remained tensed.

"It's okay," Tara continued. "I'm not here to hurt you." Slowly, carefully, she slipped her hand through the bars. "Peace, little one."

The bony shoulders underneath the sweatshirt seemed to relax slightly.

Tara's fingers reached the back of one of the child's large hands. She began to stroke it gently. At the first touch, the boy convulsed, shrinking away from Tara and balling himself even smaller.

"You're all right; I won't hurt you." Tara continued to whisper soothingly, and slowly the boy unfolded himself, though he continued to look away from the direction of her voice. Tara again began to stroke his hand, which lay relaxed by his head. It twitched at her touch, but did not withdraw.

"Peace little one. Jesus loves you."

The hand was still relaxed. Dark green eyes flicked up to Tara's face and then back down. Tara smiled. Gradually, the boy lifted his other hand and moved it next to the one Tara was stroking. His eyes met Tara's as she began to stroke that hand, and the corners of the boy's mouth turned up.

"Master, we would have attacked if we could," Doubt said anxiously.

"I know, my demon," Satan growled deep in his throat, glaring at the cowering demon twisting and tossing on the floor. The dark one turned, sinking back on his throne, and the demon relaxed.

"Today, however, you will fight," Satan ordered. *"Fear saw a legion of angels enter my realm. They will be at the orphanage when you get there. Tell all the other servants of darkness to rally around you."*

Becky had a headache, but she smiled as she watched Tara and the little boy. She turned to Graham and George. A signal seemed to go off between them, and they all reached into the bag, pulling out different toys.

Becky approached a child dressed in pink sweatpants and a purple shirt. One of her eyes was so swollen that only a fringe of eyelash was visible. "Hello, sweetie," Becky cooed. Like the boy Tara had approached, the little girl cringed into a ball.

"The darkness seems to grow greater," Strength whispered to Unity as they traveled toward Turkey.

Unity looked up and saw a dark splotch that smeared itself across the land. It smelled of fear and bitterness and swirled sickly as the orphanage came into view.

"If only the people would surrender their false worship and turn to our Lord, the darkness would clear," Strength said. His face grew stern as they approached the churning mass.

The angels were all used to working in the darkness, but Unity thought it was more concentrated now than when they had left the orphanage the day before.

Shining even brighter with the presence of the Lord's Spirit, they entered the dark, and it melted away, shriveling into a clear path for the angels to follow. They advanced, but Unity could see shadowy figures on either side of them, slinking about with menacing eyes in the dark smog. Suddenly, Unity yelped. A burning feeling from his stomach seemed to swallow him, and as he fell, a cackle pierced the air. The last thing Unity saw were the twisted feet of a demon.

Chapter 12

The boy whose hands Tara had stroked clasped the stuffed rabbit and waved it around, making happy noises. Graham had lifted a little girl from her crib and was cradling her in his arms. Across the room, George was bending over a child, smiling and making a teddy bear dance around him. Becky stood by the crib of the girl with the swollen eye, wondering what to do next.

As Unity disappeared in front of them, the angels began to cry out everywhere. Demons cackled as five more angels fell to the ground and disappeared.

"Angels!" cried Strength. "Rally for the glory of God!"

Flames burst around the celestials as they drew their swords, and like one they lurched forward into the fringe of darkness. Grace whipped out his weapon and pierced a demon through the chest, but as that demon melted away, another one leaped into his place. Grace thrust his sword in the demon's direction but the demon blocked, twisting his own weapon so that he and Grace were locked face-to-face.

"Really, angel, don't you think your master is overreacting?" Spite snarled. "There are so many more important things happening in the world. What use are retarded children? They are curses, are they not? Just burdens that their families must put up with. What use are your battles here, angel?"

"Not one sparrow falls from the sky without the Lord's notice," countered Grace. "How much more does he notice the lives of these little children?"

"What lives?" the demon shrieked. "There is no life here!"

"Exactly. But Jesus came to give them life, and that more abundantly."
Grace lunged forward, unlocking his sword from around Spite's weapon
and plunging it into the demon's stomach.

Strength shouted above the melee, "Press forward to the
orphanage!"

Orphanage workers gathered in the doorway and watched the
proceedings curiously. They murmured to each other as more and
more children focused their eyes on the four Americans. A few weak
giggles came from some of the cribs.

Suddenly, there was a mournful howl from the back of the
room.

The angels finally pushed their way to the door of the handicapped
building and burst in. There were demons inside waiting for them.

"Divide like planned!" Strength commanded. "His Spirit will help
us!"

The moaning grew louder. Becky tried to see where it was
coming from, but she had to stop a moment to lean against a wall;
her headache was making her dizzy.

Grace and his companions burst into the room and began to fight
through the demons.

"Holy, holy, holy is the Lord God Almighty!" shouted Justice as
another demon melted away in front of him.

The other angels repeated the cry until the whole room and the rooms
beyond rang with it. "Holy, holy, holy is the Lord God Almighty!"

Becky shook her head as the dizziness eased, and she approached the crib of the crying girl. Her arms and legs were tied to the sides of her crib with scarves that were stained brownish red. She was shaking back and forth, straining against her bonds, and whipping her head around wildly. *Oh, boy,* Becky thought. *Lord, please help.*

As the child's head whipped back and forth, Grace caught glimpses of dark, twisted features moving in sync with her head. As her arms tensed, a pair of twisted limbs braced against the same bonds. The girl opened her mouth and howled mournfully, and although Becky heard the cries of a little girl, Grace heard the delighted shriek of a demon who was relishing every moment he possessed her.

"My Spirit is with you, Grace," came the Lord's voice, and the angel's sword roared through the darkness that hovered around the child.

The demon stopped his shriek and glared at Grace. His eyes shone blood red and a smile twisted around his face. He rose from the child, hovering just above her. "All that for one child," he sneered, gesturing at the flames that licked the air around the sword. "All for just one lowly child whose brain is gone and who doesn't have a soul to care for her."

"Exactly," Grace said for the second time that day. This time when he struck, the demon dodged and sank back into the child. He howled, his voice breaking through the child's whimpers.

Becky's heart beat frantically as the girl began to shriek again and struggle against the bonds more wildly than ever, jerking around and around. Her eyes grew wide as she watched the scarves around the girl's wrists and ankles turning red. Gasping, Becky realized that it was the girl's blood.

"Demon, you have no place here!" Grace shouted, and he thrust the pillar of flames forward, catching the demon off guard and plunging it

into his chest. The demon howled in pain for a moment and then was gone, leaving only a lingering stench of evil.

The girl stopped struggling and fell limp, her eyes closed. Her chest heaved slowly, and her eyes opened.

"There you are," Becky said cheerfully, shaking the stuffed elephant in front of the girl's face. The girl watched the elephant romp across her vision, and she giggled weakly.

"Well done, Grace," came the Father's voice.

Chapter 13

A week later, Graham, Becky, and George arrived back in Arizona, and Becky immediately drove the fifteen minutes to her daughter Amy's house. Becky breathed in the cool air inside the house. She was very thankful for air conditioning after working in the hot windowless rooms of the orphanage.

Amy closed the dishwasher. "Now, I've been waiting to hear *all* about your trip!"

Becky followed her daughter into the living room. She felt like she could talk for hours. She told Amy about how they had quickly emptied the duffel bags and managed to wipe some of the hard snot from the kids' faces. "Mr. Kavur told us that the children were not only physically handicapped but also extremely retarded. Vegetables, he called them. But after the first day, the kids began to wave their stuffed animals in the air whenever we came into the room. I knew then that severe retardation isn't the case."

"You mentioned on the phone that one little girl really took to Dad," Amy said. "What did the workers think of you nicknaming her Giggles?"

"They kept their distance the whole time. Not that they were rude; they just seemed suspicious and extremely puzzled. Tara said it was because we were doing something so out of the ordinary from what they are used to. They simply couldn't understand why we want to help these kids. And they are so poor themselves. The state doesn't provide much money to care for the kids, never mind to pay the workers. So they focus on being able to feed and care for their own families. Some mornings, we'd arrive at the orphanage and realize that many of the toys we handed out the day before were missing.

Tara explained that the toys were probably at the workers' homes, with *their* kids.

"Before we left, we gave Tara the funds to hire two Turkish believers to work in the handicapped building every day. And we put a bathtub and a hot-water heater in the bathroom so the kids can get warm water for baths. . . . And, oh, Amy, that other room I told you about." Becky paused and shuddered. "I had nightmares. The lifeless eyes of the kids in that one room followed me home at night. Your dad and George called it the Vomit Room, because when one of the kids threw up, others crawled all over the floor to eat the mess."

Amy looked down. "So are you and Dad going to do anything else with this orphanage?"

"You know, Amy, we're both praying about it, and I think we're going to see if anyone is interested in going back with us for a second trip."

Amy smiled. "Oh, Mom, this is what you and Dad have wanted to do for so long! I could never do anything like that."

Becky was amazed as the ministry to the children of the orphanage grew. The second trip to the orphanage was the first of many more. Hug Teams, volunteers to love on the orphans one-on-one, were formed to travel to the orphanage. Adam decided to get involved with his parents' ministry, and soon he was leading as many Hug Team trips as Becky.

The children responded well to each visit, but the conditions of the orphanage were too harsh to change overnight. With every Hug Team trip, Becky learned that one or two of the children had starved to death since the last team's visit. Even after Becky and Graham hired the two Turkish believers who now worked in the orphanage full-time, there was never enough food or time to feed all the children.

Graham and Becky decided to formalize what they were doing by starting a nonprofit organization, Least of These Ministries. The name came from Matthew 25:40: "The King will reply, 'I tell you the truth, whatever you did for one of the least of these brothers of mine, you did for me.'" As news of the ministry grew, people began to send money for improvements in the handicapped building. The ministry was able to renovate other bathrooms, clean and paint hallways, and remodel the kitchen.

When they decided to redo the Vomit Room, Becky was alarmed to hear that the renovations would cost fifteen thousand dollars. She called Graham, afraid of what he might say. She was thrilled to hear him respond, "That's all right, honey. If we have to take another mortgage on our house to pay for it, that's what we'll do."

But before their desire to redo the Vomit Room had been made known to anyone, Becky and Graham received a check for the exact amount they needed from a man who had just heard of Least of These Ministries. Becky contacted Alan Grant to see if he wanted to help with the renovations. Not only did he say yes, but he recruited a team that eventually flew with him to the orphanage. Wood floors and carpet replaced the chewed-up linoleum; the holes in the walls were fixed and the walls painted bright yellow; and Becky and a Hug Team bought high chairs and toys. The Vomit Room became the Hope Room.

Becky could see that God was making his presence known in more and more ways as Least of These continued to step out in faith. Becky and Tara found a boy named Levent, whose legs had turned black and painfully prevented him from walking. Becky asked the orphanage doctor to look at Levent, but the doctor refused to do anything in the Vomit Room. That night, a Christian doctor visited

Tara's house. Tara and Becky brought him to the orphanage the next day, but when they found Levent, he was sitting up and his legs were no longer black.

"Well, I don't know what happened!" Becky exclaimed.

"Seriously, Dr. Reynolds, this boy couldn't move yesterday," Tara said. She was surprised too.

"Well," Dr. Reynolds said, "Did you pray for him yesterday?"

"Of course."

"There you go, then!" He smiled and winked. "You know, prayer really does work."

Becky and Tara looked back at Levent, who was comfortably gazing around the room with his one good eye. The two women looked at each other and began to laugh. "You'd think we'd know that by now!"

Tara had met one seventeen-year-old boy who had never been taken out of his crib. One day as she stroked his stiff legs, she told him about God. "God loves you, Mustafa," she said quietly in Turkish.

"Oh, no, God can't love me," said the boy. "I'm crippled."

"He doesn't care if you're crippled. He loves—"

"No, he doesn't," the boy insisted. "No one can love me, because I'm crippled. I've been cursed."

When Tara went home that night, she prayed, asking God to reveal himself to Mustafa no matter how long it took. The next morning, Tara visited Mustafa again and immediately noticed a change in his countenance. He smiled brightly when she walked over to him and held his head higher than she had ever seen him do. Softly, she told him, "God loves you, little one."

Mustafa grinned and replied, "I know he does. Jesus sat by my crib last night and told me!"

Chapter 14

B ahar rolled over on the comforter.

She still hadn't gotten used to feeling the cold, hard floor underneath her. She looked up at the crib, longing to be back inside it. The bars of the crib would protect her from the rodents that now scurried across her face at night.

A small, wrinkled hand appeared between the bars of the crib, and her little brother, Ashar, began to wail, like he always did when he was awake. Bahar rolled over again, clasping her hands over her ears.

Presently, the bedroom door opened. Bahar's hands were suddenly jerked away from her head, and Nimet pulled her upright. "What are you doing to your little brother, eh?" she shouted. "I leave you alone and what do you do?" Nimet's eyes were bleary, and she shook Bahar by the arms as she yelled.

Bahar's eyes grew wide with fear.

"You grow jealous because he took your crib, don't you?" Nimet continued. "And here you lay all day because you are too lazy to learn to walk! What do you expect me to do with you? Why does Allah curse me with a crippled child? You are useless! Useless!"

Bahar could no longer hear what Nimet was saying because of Ashar's wails.

Hope watched painfully, his fists clenched. "He who is the Ancient of Days has a greater plan," he reminded himself.

"It's time," the dark one said to the demons in front of him. "My enemy has done much to declare his glory; however, we must make sure that the glory from Bahar is taken from him forever."

"My lord," said Strife, "we will take great pleasure in following your command."

Despair and Fear grinned. Then all three demons disappeared to do their master's bidding.

Satan sat still for a long time after they were gone. Something was nagging at him. He had a feeling that what he was about to do wouldn't work the way he wanted it to. Did his enemy already know what he was up to?

"But how could he get glory out of pain that I inflict?" Satan's laugh was full of venom. "That question has puzzled humans for centuries, and I will continue to use it to my advantage."

❦

"You have returned, dark one?" the Lord said.

Satan's mouth cracked into a smile, and he crouched into the corner.

"Have you seen the orphanage?" the Lord continued. "The people in your stronghold are praising me now."

Cautiously, Satan laughed, "You have done much that I did not expect you to do."

"Yet you laugh."

The dark folds of Satan's cloak billowed and shivered. "Yes, I do, and I can only assume that you, mighty and powerful one that you are, already know why I laugh."

The Lord's face shone brilliantly, but his eyes seemed clouded with sadness.

Satan laughed again. "You see it, don't you? Bahar has been overlooked in your enthusiasm over your pitiful, self-sacrificing servants. While you've been busy with the orphans and the Bateses, I have been chiseling away at what little life Bahar and her family have. They are too far gone now." He spit out the words like they were poison, and he stood upright now, away from the wall. "You have brought your name glory, no doubt, but now your greater glory through Bahar has been taken. It will go to me." Satan cackled and was gone.

The Lord watched the smoky vapor his enemy left behind. Now the shadow of sadness in his face melted away, and he smiled. Satan had overlooked one thing: he was contending with God.

Chapter 15

The lights from the cars danced in Bahar's eyes. The strange voices she heard also made her afraid. She dug her fingers into the shirt of the man who was holding her. The lights were so bright, and who were all these men? They were saying things that Bahar did not understand. "The scene . . . weapon . . . find her closest family."

Something had happened that Bahar couldn't quite grasp. Everything about the night seemed fuzzy and blurred.

"Easy, little one," whispered Hope. "It will be okay." His sword was unsheathed as he eyed the demons scurrying around, laughing at him crazily.

Bahar gazed at the open door of her house. She hadn't seen her little brother come through that door yet. Where was he? When she saw him last, he was still crying, crying because her mother had hurt him.

Bahar had been sitting on the floor, playing with Ashar, when Nimet stumbled into the room with a hazy look on her face. Bahar watched in horror as Nimet caught Ashar by the arm and began to scream and shout. The next minute, Ashar was crying in pain. Bahar saw anger in her mother's eyes, but she couldn't understand why she was hurting Ashar.

Then Sakir walked in.

"*Nimet!*" he roared, anger hot on his face and in his voice. He stalked across the room and opened a drawer. Then there was a *bang!*

emma's STORY

Hope's eyes filled with compassion as he watched the little girl relive the evening in her mind.

A demon from behind the police officer holding Bahar stared at Hope for a moment and then ran into the house, laughing with malice. Hope's sword twitched in his hand, but the Lord had warned him not to attack Satan's servants unless they tried to touch Bahar.

Bahar stared into the flashing lights on the car and grasped the dark blue shirt even tighter.

There had been a sickening silence after the shot. For one moment, her father had looked as if he was about to shout again; then he had stalked into the bedroom and slammed the door. Soon the sirens had come, and the cars with the bright lights. Now, as Bahar watched the open doorway again, she saw her father coming out of the house with his hands behind him, followed closely by a policeman.

"Father!" she cried, reaching toward Sakir. But he didn't even look up as the officer shoved him into the back of a car, or as it drove away.

"You fool!" Despair shrieked after Sakir. "You thought it would feel good to get rid of her, didn't you? But now you feel guilty; now you will be punished. Now your children will be taken away from you! What do you have left now, fool?"

The officer tightened his hold on Bahar as she reached for her father. "How long will it take to find other family members?" he asked. "And the boy—has he been taken to the hospital?"

"Yes, sir, he has."

"A few hours at least to find her closest relatives," someone else said.

"I'll take her to the station, then," said the officer holding Bahar. She felt him sigh. "This whole situation is bad," he said.

"Oh, yes, such a shame," Strife agreed sarcastically. "The poor, innocent children."

Hysterical laughter erupted among the demons, and Hope watched grimly as they danced around together. He sheathed his sword and followed the officer climbing into the car to go to the station. Suddenly, a small smile relaxed the angel's features, and he whispered into the dark, "Enjoy this small triumph while you can, fallen ones."

Eventually, the police located Bahar's grandparents. The officer who had taken Bahar to the station now drove to the grandparents' home and knocked on the door.

An old man opened it only slightly. "Yes, what do want?" he asked gruffly. Then he saw Bahar in the officer's arms and waved the officer into the front room. Bahar's grandmother appeared behind her husband.

Bahar had only seen her grandparents three times in her life, but they had always been a comforting sight to her. Halime was big and silent, but his eyes shone whenever he saw his grandchildren. Ulma's skin was the color of cinnamon, and her eyes were kind. A plain head cloth covered her hair and most of her wrinkled forehead.

The officer explained what had happened. "A neighbor called us immediately after hearing the gunshot. But when we arrived at the house, your daughter had already passed from life. We did all that was in our power."

Bahar saw tears running down Ulma's face, though she kept her head bowed and was silent.

emma's STORY

"And what of my grandson?" Halime asked.

"He was taken to the hospital to be treated for his injuries. We'll contact you later about him. There will be papers to sign." The officer placed Bahar into Halime's arms.

"May Allah grant her mercy," Halime said quietly, passing Bahar to his wife, "but I had a feeling that something like this would happen."

"Oh, Halime," Grandmother whispered to her husband, sitting down in a chair and shifting Bahar to her lap.

"Allah will give us strength, Ulma. Do not worry."

Ulma nodded and took a deep breath and looked at Bahar. "Well, my little one," she said in a shaky voice, "where shall we put you for tonight?"

Bahar looked into her grandmother's tear-filled eyes. Halime's face seemed carved of hard gray stone. There was no comfort in either of them.

Later that night, as Bahar lay in bed in a dark room, she thought she heard someone crying.

⁘

"Mrs. Bates, can I help you?" asked Ahmed, the new middle-aged driver for Least of These, as Becky began hauling bags of oatmeal from the back of his van onto a cart to take into the handicapped building.

"Oh, thank you, Ahmed, but I don't think you want to come in. The kids are really different in there; you wouldn't like it."

"No, please, Mrs. Bates. I'd like to help."

"Are you sure?"

"Yes, I would like to see these children that you and Graham help so much." He loaded the last few bags onto the cart.

When they reached the handicapped building, Ahmed opened the door for Becky and then followed her with the cart to the Hope Room. Becky held her breath. *Lord, how will Ahmed respond to these disfigured kids?*

As soon as the children saw Ahmed carrying the oatmeal, they began to run and crawl toward him, shouting with excitement. He stepped backward, just as Becky had feared.

Reaching over and touching him, Compassion whispered, "Be filled. The Lord is going to bless you, Ahmed."

Then, in a moment that touched Becky's heart forever, Ahmed dropped the oatmeal bags and scooped up the nearest three children, tears running down his face.

Chapter 16

"*Eat*, Bahar! *Eat!* What am I going to with you if you don't eat something? Tell me that." Ulma's wrinkled hand waved a spoon in front of Bahar's mouth, tempting her. "Come on, silly girl, please. My dinner is getting cold because of you. *Eat, eat!*"

"Give it up for now, Ulma." Sitting across the table from Ulma and Bahar, Halime sighed. "She will eat when she gets hungry."

Ulma set the spoon back on the plate and turned away from Bahar's high chair. "Halime, she eats barely anything. Barely enough to stay alive! She used to eat for Nimet, did she not?"

The air in the room suddenly became thick and quiet.

"I am sorry, Halime," Ulma murmured. She clasped her hands in her lap and stared at them.

The old man grunted and turned a page of his newspaper. It had been three months since their daughter had been killed; he still did not like her name mentioned.

"Bahar stood up by herself today," Ulma said, to change the subject.

Halime nodded slowly. "She is getting much stronger under your good care, my wife—even though she eats like a small bird."

Hope watched Bahar stare blankly at the other side of the room. "Please, Bahar, eat something," he whispered in her ear.

Ulma saw Bahar look down at the spoon sitting on her plate, but she said nothing.

"Give it up, angel."

Hope recoiled inwardly at the oily words. It was Despair.

"Trying to salvage what's left of her?" the demon continued, gesturing toward Bahar.

"She's already been saved," Hope answered.

"She has?" Despair asked. He clacked his claws together. "Maybe she was saved from dying, but that's only because my master lost interest in her after we looked at that brain of hers. It's fried. Seems that life with those parents and then seeing her mother shot was too much for her."

Hope didn't reply.

"You can't ignore me forever, angel," Despair hissed. "Something's happening now that your master is not prepared for, and no pitiful celestial attempt can stop it."

"Whatever plan the dark one may have, the Lord already knows and is prepared for it," Hope replied, his sword blazing to life. "Now go."

The demon eyed Hope's sword warily. "I have better things to do than fight you, angel. Besides, it's too late now. I hope you are ready for what's coming."

Ulma and Bahar were both staring at the spoon on Bahar's plate. It was humming. As they watched it, the humming got louder. The spoon began to bounce, as did the plate. The basket of fruit by Bahar's head began to swing.

"*Eeeeek!*" shrieked Ulma. "The ground is moving!"

Hope looked out the window and saw a crowd of demons dancing and cackling in the street.

Bahar watched as every dish on the table began to vibrate and shake right off the table, shattering onto the floor. Books fell off shelves; pictures slid off walls to the floor, the glass shooting across the room. A sound like a large truck rumbled through the kitchen.

Halime and Ulma stood up, knocking their chairs to the ground. "Quick, Ulma!" Halime shouted above the roar. "Get Bahar and get outside!"

"Where are you going?" she shrieked, turning to Bahar and lifting her from the high chair.

"I must get our money. Take our grandchild!"

Halime rushed into the other room. Bahar began to wail as Ulma yanked her free from the highchair. Suddenly, a tremor ran through the floor, sending Ulma stumbling into a wall. She dropped Bahar, and Bahar screamed louder. The chain above the basket of fruit snapped, and oranges and melons bounced across the room, their juice squirting everywhere. The glass in a window shattered.

Hope jabbed the basket with his shoulder, knocking it away from Ulma and Bahar, and deflected the shards of window glass with his sword. He heard demons laughing.

Ulma scrambled back to her feet and picked up Bahar. "Halime!" she screamed over the deafening roar. "HALIME!"

There was no answer.

Suddenly, a crack sprawled up the wall next to Ulma and Bahar. It spit out chunks of plaster, and the ground seemed to rise like a wave.

"Ulma!" came a cry down the hall.

"Halime!" Ulma screamed and stumbled toward the hall.

"Ulma! Get—*aauurgh!*"

The ceiling in the hall collapsed as the floor heaved again.

"HALIME!" Ulma turned toward the front door; it was hanging by one hinge. She threw herself against the wall to try to keep from falling as she made her way to the door. "Allah be merciful," she panted.

Ulma and Bahar were sobbing and coughing. Chunks of ceiling flew through the air, and plaster dust was everywhere.

A piece of ceiling hurtled through the air toward Bahar, and Hope stepped into its path, searing it in half with his sword.

There was a ripping sound; a huge crack in the ceiling, and then in a shower of dust and plaster, everything went dark.

Venomous laughter echoed across the air.

C﹏ﾗ

"Graham, Becky, Amy, you'd better come look at this," Mark Sneed said as he hung up the phone and switched on the TV. Everyone, even the grandchildren, got up from the table and gathered around.

Becky gasped. An earthquake had hit Turkey in the region of the orphanage. The news video showed collapsed buildings, sinking cars, and people wandering haphazardly through the streets.

"Grandma, will the orphanage be okay?" asked Becca, one of Mark and Amy's twins.

"I hope so, darlin'," Becky said. *Oh, Lord,* she prayed, *please have your way in this.*

C﹏ﾗ

Hope could see no sign of life anywhere in the rubble that had been Ulma and Halime's home. Demons crawled through the ruined buildings all around him, but none came near.

Sometimes, Hope could not understand the Lord's will. How did something like this work out to proclaim his name, reveal his glory, and show his love?

Strength and Justice came to Hope's side. Their robes were torn from battle, but their weapons still blazed, and fire still glinted in their eyes.

"Hope, come join us," said Strength. "There's nothing more you can do here."

Hope nodded. As he followed them away from the ruins of the house, he gripped his sword tighter. It was time to fight.

Chapter 17

A my turned from the sink as Becky came in the kitchen door. She thought her mom looked especially tired. "Come and sit down," she said. "I'll get you some iced tea."

"Thanks, sweetie," Becky replied. "I can't quite catch my breath today." She lowered herself into a chair at the table. "I feel like I've been running a marathon."

Amy brought two glasses of tea to the table and sat down with her mom. "So is the Hug Team trip still on?" she asked.

Becky sipped her tea and shook her head. "We'll have to postpone it. The orphanage wasn't affected by the earthquake, but the government is limiting tourism until the damage from the earthquake is under control. The U.S. has sent rescue dogs along with workers and supplies."

"Did you get to talk to Ahmed?"

"Yes, and he said that postponing would be fine."

"He's doing a good job for you now as coordinator as well as driver, isn't he?"

"Yes, and he takes such good care of each team we send over there. You'll love him, Amy. His English has really improved too."

"I'm sure I will, and I'm glad you were finally able to talk to him about the trip and get the timing straightened out," Amy said. "Maybe this sounds selfish, but I was getting nervous about going anyway, so this gives me more time to prepare myself."

Becky laughed. "Oh, Amy, you know there's nothing to worry about. We just go and love on the kids a bit."

"I know, Mom, but I do feel inadequate. I've never worked with handicapped kids, and I'm not sure I'll know what to do. . . . I sound ridiculous, don't I? You'd think after growing up with you as my mother I wouldn't worry about anything new or unfamiliar."

"Maybe it's your father in you," Becky grinned, her eyes twinkling.

"But he married the wrong person to let fear of the unfamiliar stop him! You and Dad have been so amazing with Least of These. Mark and I are really excited about going over and seeing all of the work that's been done."

"We're excited too, Amy. And hopefully, we'll be able to get back into the country in the next few months and actually take you there."

"I hope so. It must be so hard over there right now. I wonder how this is going to affect the orphanage."

Becky nodded. "I've been wondering too."

When Hope was next summoned to the holy court, the Lord smiled, but Hope could feel his sadness. The earthquake had affected him in the way that always puzzled Hope. He knew God loved these people that he had created, and he was completely in control, yet he allowed them to be hurt, and it brought him pain.

"You have a question?" the Lord said.

Hope was again amazed. "I do."

"Ask it then."

"I can't see how this story will work out." Hope lifted his gaze and saw that the Lord was smiling.

"Must you know every word of the story before I reveal it?"

Hope knew that he did not.

The Lord's eyes filled with more sadness, but he said, "Bahar's story is not over, and she will soon know my love."

Hope looked up, rejoicing.

"She was buried beneath the rubble and suffers much," the Lord said. "Now, it is time for you to return to my child."

Bahar woke up coughing. When she tried to open her eyes, the dust stung and sent tears down her cheeks.

"Grandpa?" she squeaked. "Grandma?"

No sound.

"Grandma?" she tried again.

Still there was no answer.

"Easy, little one," Hope whispered. "Just hold on."

He watched as Bahar's dark eyes filled with fear and pain, and her little hand clutched a piece of fabric sticking out from a rock by her head. She was so silent. Hope knew that the next few days would be very hard.

Chapter 18

After three days of darkness and discomfort, suddenly Bahar saw light streak into her miniature tomb. Her eyes stung and she blinked. There was movement somewhere above her, and she heard sniffing sounds. Then a black nose blocked the light.

"Come on," Hope encouraged the owner of the nose. "Let him know what you've found."

The nose disappeared, and a deep, clear bark pierced the air. Words that Bahar couldn't understand answered the bark. "Eh? Whatcha got there, girl?"

Then a pair of icy blue eyes shaded by a cap blocked the light. Bahar heard static and then more words that sounded strange to her ears. "I got another one here. Small kid, can't tell how old. Pinned under rubble. Can't tell if there's injury."

The eyes remained fixed on Bahar, and she stared back.

"You just sit tight, there, honey. It'll be all right," the voice said, soothingly. "And man, that's one solemn face you got. No wonder, after what you've been through, poor thing."

Despair watched the scene angrily. "I thought she died," he hissed.

Chaos appeared at his side. "What are you mumbling about?"

Despair growled, resisting the urge to attack Chaos. "Nothing, sir," he said. "I had hoped that we killed her. But she's still alive."

Chaos laughed provokingly. "Your mind is weak, Despair," he said.

"Can you not see how keeping her alive will rob the enemy of even more of his glory? Where is her father?"

"In jail."

"And her grandparents?"

"Dead."

"And will her uncle, her only living relative, take her into his home as damaged as her brain is?" Chaos asked gleefully.

"I think I'm beginning to see," said Despair. "There's no place left for her to go but the orphanage. Yes, perfect! A place of hopelessness even greater than her parents' home. . . . Yes, this will be perfect."

"Took you long enough to see. If you understood our master's ways better, you might be as high in his favor as I am," Chaos said before he disappeared, leaving behind the stench of death.

Hope had heard everything. The pieces of the story were beginning to fit together. Bahar, the orphanage, Becky and Graham . . . Was the Almighty going to bring them all together for his glory?

The hinges of the small metal door squealed in protest as the social worker entered the handicapped building. Spiderwebs hung heavily in the corners of the small reception room, and bits of fallen ceiling plaster were scattered across the cracked linoleum floor. In one corner of the room, mold poked over the edge of a stool.

A wispy-haired woman glanced up from behind the desk and nodded to the man with the child in his arms. "This is the one from the earthquake?" she asked.

"Yes."

The woman sniffed and ran a hand over her nose. She opened a drawer and took out a large, worn book. "Name?"

"Bahar Yilmaz."

"Any living relatives?"

"She has a father, but he's in prison. She can't go there. Custody was given to an uncle, but he refused to take her. . . . There's no one left, so we brought her here."

The woman nodded, sighing. "All right then. Age?"

"Her uncle wasn't sure. I don't know, three, maybe, or four?"

The woman glanced up at the social worker and raised an eyebrow. "You don't know?"

Shoving a couple of crumpled pages at the woman, the social worker answered, "This was all they could find. There are three birth certificates, all with different dates. I have no idea why. . . . You know how it is."

The woman scanned the papers quickly, and her eyebrow raised again. "We've seen worse," she said.

She entered Bahar's name and age into the book and shoved the papers into a drawer. "Three it is," she pronounced. She stood up, wiped her hands on her stained apron, and took Bahar from the social worker. "Thank you."

The man nodded and left, the door screeching after him.

Bahar's head began to buzz as the woman carried her down a hallway. Where was she? Who was this woman? She stiffened as the smells and sounds of the building permeated the hallway. Where was she going?

"I'm sorry, Bahar," Hope whispered. "This is where you must be right now." His sword was drawn, and he glared a warning to the demons looking on.

Chapter 19

Once the government opened up the country to tourism again, the Hug Teams were able to resume their work at the orphanage.

"Okay, team, everyone in here," Becky called, beckoning the line of people into the Hope Room. "Ahmed will pick us up in about four hours to take us to lunch, and we've got a lot of kids to feed and love on until then. There's the kitchen door, you three."

Three men filed into the kitchen, carrying large boxes.

"Ann and Mary," Becky continued, "if you two could follow them and start making the oatmeal, that would be great. The rest of you, divide up into teams to scoop the oatmeal into the bowls—second cupboard on the left, sweetheart—and pass them to others to hand-feed the kids. Remember, everyone, don't set the bowls down, or else the kids will dog pile to get at them."

Becky reached down and held the hand of the little girl waving at her, "Oh, hello, Merve. Are you ready to eat, sweetie?" She cooed at her for a few minutes.

When Becky stood up, she found that she couldn't catch her breath, and her vision went blank for several long moments. *Wonder what that's about?* she thought. But she forgot about it as she walked into the kitchen and began to help with the oatmeal.

In a few minutes, the room was bustling like a cafeteria.

Amy grabbed a bowl of warm oatmeal and scanned the room. She had heard all of Graham and Becky's stories; she had seen photos and videos of the children and of this place where they lived. But she had decided that nothing except actually walking down the halls, smelling the smells, and interacting with the children would allow her to fully understand what this place was and what Least of These did. And now she was here. Children were jumping and shaking their heads with excitement between bites, there were shrieks of laughter everywhere, and one little girl was crying, "Ma-ma-ma-ma-mah! Ma-ma-ma-ma-mah!"

Amy smiled and made her way to a corner of the room where there were fewer adults. In this quieter portion of the room, children and blankets and toys were piled like small mountains. A splotch of brown curls caught her eye. Most of the children here were shaved bald because that made it easier to keep them clean, but this child still had her hair. She appeared to be one of the more severely mentally handicapped kids; her gaze was unfocused and she didn't seem to notice the commotion going on around her.

"Hey, sweetie," Amy said, sitting down on the floor and reaching for her.

The instant that her fingers touched the worn flannel of the little girl's zipped-up pajamas and stroked the tangled curls away from her pale face, she knew. This was a moment she would remember forever. "Dear God!" she whispered. There was something about this child. Amy lifted a spoonful of oatmeal to the child's lips, but that seemed somehow not enough. She put down the spoon and placed the child in her lap. The girl whimpered and flinched, but slowly relaxed. The clamor in the rest of the room seemed to fade. *God, what's going on?* Amy prayed.

Hope beamed over Amy's shoulder, watching her cradle Bahar in her arms. "Holy is the Lord God Almighty," he whispered.

"Did any of you see that little girl with the curls?" Mark asked as Ahmed drove the team back to the hotel that evening.

Amy sighed. The little girl had beautiful eyes, but the vacant look in them hadn't changed the entire time Amy had tried to feed her.

"I noticed her too, and I saw you feeding her for a while, Amy," said Becky. "She really stands out."

"She does," Amy agreed. She wasn't ready to talk about the connection she felt with the little girl.

⁂

The girl's name was Bahar, Amy learned the next day from Delar, the wispy-haired woman at the front desk of the handicapped building. Her father had shot her mother, and she lost her grandparents in the earthquake. When the Hug Team took a break from feeding, Amy decided to revisit the little girl. She found her in a red crib in a room just down the hall from the Hope Room.

"Hello, Bahar," she whispered, smiling at the empty brown eyes. The little girl whimpered softly and her hand twitched, but when Amy reached down to stroke it, Bahar flinched.

Oh, Lord, Amy prayed, *to think of the trauma this child must have gone through . . .*

Sunlight shone through the windows that a previous Hug Team had scraped and cleaned. It played across Bahar's crib, lighting her hair into a golden brown, and making her skin look even paler.

"All right, team," Becky called from the door of the room. "It's time for the next lunch shift." She walked to where Amy stood. "This girl really stands out," she said again.

Grace and Strength watched mother and daughter from a distance.
"They feel his Spirit speaking to them," Strength said.
"Another door opens," said Grace.

That night the Hug Team went to dinner at a local restaurant. Although they enjoyed the fellowship of the other Hug Team members, Amy and Mark decided to sit with Amy's parents.

"So, what about this new little girl?" Graham asked. "Delar said that she's an earthquake victim."

"She told me that too," Amy said. "Her name is Bahar."

"It looks like the poor thing is suffering from post-traumatic stress," Becky commented. "We've seen it in a few of the children, but none of them have seemed so freshly traumatized as her."

"I think we need to help that little girl in a special way," Mark said.

Amy stared at her husband, usually so quiet.

"It's only natural," Mark went on. "I mean, if it's not too late to possibly save her, then we should do what we can to help."

"Who knows what we could be in for if we decide to do that," Graham said.

"God knows," Becky answered, "and if it's something we really feel like he wants us to do . . . I don't know about the rest of you, but I haven't been able to get this little girl out of my mind since we saw her."

Mark put his fork down and looked around at the table. "I don't know about you," he said, "but I don't want to stand before God someday knowing that we should have helped this little girl but we ignored the calling."

Chapter 20

"*You* have disappointed me, Despair." The dark one's voice shuddered.

Despair resisted the shudder and stared at the floor. Even there he saw fumes of his master's displeasure.

"Your orders were clear and simple," Satan wheezed. "And there was nothing but one angel to stop you. Why did you not obey me?"

"I thought she was dead, my lord."

"You thought?" Satan repeated. "But did you know? Did you know for sure that she was dead?"

"I thought—"

"You should have known for sure!" Satan hissed, leaning forward from his throne. "Is that too much to ask? After you and my other faithful servants deceive peoples' minds by making them believe that what they THINK must be TRUTH?"

"But Chaos said—"

"Silence!" Satan roared. "YOU should have known better! During your time in my service, you have constantly sowed deceit into the humans who have lost faith in my enemy. Surely YOU could not fall for such an old trick! And yet you did." The dark lord leaned even further out of his seat, twisting and writhing hypnotically. Despair was reminded of the first deception his master achieved over the humans, when their world had just begun.

"You let your pride and overconfidence blind you to the power of my enemy," Satan spat. A deep burning feeling made Despair clench his jaw in pain.

"His angels are nothing," Satan continued. "They can be defeated. But the one they call lord . . . You should know that he is not like other *celestials. His rules are not your rules; his plans are not your plans. Pride, above all else, will bring you to your knees before him!" Satan's claws twitched, and his eyes burned so deeply that Despair began to shake and whimper. "And you do not—" Satan hissed, "—want to be found there."*

Despair gave a pain-stricken cry and fell onto the floor, thrashing and twisting before Satan's penetrating gaze until, after several moments, he went limp.

"Get up," the dark master ordered. "Do not let this loss dishearten you, my fallen one. Somehow, we will turn it for my glory. Although my enemy's children have found Bahar, remember that the orphanage is still my stronghold. I have more followers there than my enemy does. My forces are still strong, and we must build them against Bahar. Attack that pitiful angel who guards her so faithfully, and the conditions in the orphanage will do the rest, just as they have done to the others there."

Despair scrambled to his feet, relief filling him.

Satan smiled at the demon before him. "You made a mistake, Despair, but I will not forget that you are one of my most faithful servants. You were one of the first to join me in the Rebellion." Satan rubbed his claws together. "This is your chance to regain my favor. And I will assign demons for you to command, and you will lead us on this great victory over our enemy."

Despair grinned at the prospect and bowed.

"Now go, but be ready for my orders to come to you soon." Satan's eyes burned gleefully. "My enemy will soon realize that I have many tricks he has not anticipated."

When the Hug Team returned home, Amy called her friend Ruth. Although she lived several states away, Ruth was one of Amy's best friends. They talked for two hours, about Turkey and the orphanage and bathing and feeding the hungry children. Mostly, however, Amy talked about Bahar.

"There was such a presence about her, something that made me want to just pick her up and take her back home with us."

"Well, did you think about actually doing that?" Ruth asked. "Have you thought about adoption?"

"We asked," Amy sighed. "Foreigners aren't allowed to adopt the children."

"That's too bad. Under any circumstance?"

"The only exceptions would be if we had Turkish ancestors or were willing to move there and adopt her as citizens in that country."

"And I guess those options are out of the question!" Ruth laughed.

"Well, you know that if we felt called to move there, we would. But Mark and I still feel that we would really like to get help for Bahar here in the states."

"I wonder what she would be like if she could come here and get help," Ruth said.

"I wonder the same thing about all the children at the orphanage," Amy said.

"Will you go back again?" Ruth asked.

"I don't know," Amy said. "I just don't know."

Chapter 21

Three months later, Amy did what she thought she could never do; she went back to the orphanage on another Hug Team trip. With Mark and their children, she had been praying about Bahar, and the family had decided to explore every option for adopting Bahar. If the government wouldn't let them adopt Bahar, maybe Bahar's uncle could take his rightful custody and then give her to the Sneeds. As soon as they arrived in Turkey with the Hug Team, Becky and Amy arranged a meeting with Bahar's uncle, Yusuf Yilmaz, at the orphanage.

Although they exchanged friendly greetings with Mr. Yilmaz through Yasmur, their translator, before sitting down, Amy thought Mr. Yilmaz seemed irritable.

Compassion, Strength, and Patience stood on one side of the room, and Pride, Suspicion, Impatience, and Shame lurked on the other.

"And just what do you want?" Mr. Yilmaz asked. His small, suspicious eyes squinted out under long, pepper-colored eyebrows.

"As we said over the phone," Amy began, "my husband and I are interested in adopting your niece, Bahar."

Suspicion nudged Yusuf.

"Why?"

"Be honest," Compassion whispered.

"Well," Amy said, "as you know, we've been working in this orphanage for a while, and we've gotten to know your niece. We've really fallen in love with her and would like to give her a better home than she has here in the orphanage."

"Why are you coming to me? She's not my daughter."

"But according to Social Services, you are her guardian. They said that you had the opportunity to take her in after the earthquake."

"You see," Pride whispered, "they think you are some barbarian to your own niece."

"They told you that?" Mr. Yilmaz asked.

"Yes."

Mr. Yilmaz shook his head. "I could not take her because I have a family of my own," he said loudly. "We cannot provide for another child, especially a handicapped one. That is why she was sent to the orphanage."

"A soft word turns away wrath," Patience reminded the two women.

Amy smiled. "We understand completely, Mr. Yilmaz. Adding another child on such short notice would be difficult for anyone."

Mr. Yilmaz nodded in agreement after Yasmur had translated for him, but still he eyed Amy and Becky with suspicion. "If it is so difficult," Mr. Yilmaz responded, "why do you wish to take her yourself?"

Becky spoke this time. "We see a lot of potential in Bahar. She is a precious girl, and we would like to give her a better life."

"Why do you say she is precious when she is one of the cursed? The hospital says that she is retarded."

"That may be, Mr. Yilmaz, but everyone is precious in God's eyes, and we look at people the same way."

Pride cackled hideously and jabbed his companions, who all laughed with him. "Good try," he said to the angels. "You did your best—but you forget that in this place the dark one is king."

"We will win now," Impatience quipped.

Compassion reached for his sword, but Strength grabbed his arm, shaking his head.

"They told me you were Christians," Mr. Yilmaz said.

"Yes, we are," said Amy.

Compassion clenched his jaw.

Shame grinned. "And now she seals her failure."

Mr. Yilmaz grunted. "Is that why you do all of these things at the orphanage?"

"Yes," Becky answered, humbly and honestly.

"Is that why you want to adopt my niece?"

"I guess you could say that," Amy told him.

"Will you take her to the United States?"

"Yes," said Amy. She looked into Mr. Yilmaz's eyes. She thought he seemed to be wavering.

"What about your brother?" Shame whispered to Mr. Yilmaz.

Mr. Yilmaz looked at Amy. "Does Sakir know?" he grunted.

"I don't know," Amy sighed. "We haven't been allowed to speak to him."

"That doesn't matter," continued Shame. *"You always looked up to your oldest brother. Now you can make him proud. Protect his daughter from these infidels and their misguided ways."*

Mr. Yilmaz straightened. "I do not understand why you would wish to adopt a cursed child. I cannot with good conscience put her into your care."

Amy tried not to look disappointed.

"It's all right, Amy," Strength whispered.

"She is my brother's daughter," Mr. Yilmaz continued. "If he wants to give her to you, it can be his choice, not mine."

"Mr. Yilmaz!" Amy said. "We were told that Sakir can no longer make that choice. You're the only one who can. Have you seen your niece? Have you seen this place? She has become worse over the past few months. This place is killing her. If nothing is done for her, she will die, just like so many of the other children do."

The demons cackled louder.

"Calm down, Amy," Patience said. *"You won't help the situation by getting angry."*

"He doesn't even need my help now," Pride smirked. *"She has insulted his country."* The demon grinned. *"At least, our lord below has taught him to think so."*

Mr. Yilmaz stiffened. "Well, that is why you are here, isn't it?" he said indignantly. "To help these children? Then do it. If they are still dying, you are not doing enough. If you do not like the way we take care of them, then leave. They are not your concern anyway."

He stood up. "Whatever you choose to do, leave me out of it." He bowed and left the room.

The demons cackled and followed Mr. Yilmaz. Pride and Impatience lingered for a moment, but after a threatening glance from the angels, they slunk out of the room.

"Well," sighed Becky. "At least this meeting didn't get any worse."

Amy wanted to laugh at her mother's optimistic attitude, but she couldn't muster more than a half smile.

Becky put a hand on her daughter's shoulder. Her brightly manicured fingernails were just one of the many echoes of the energetic, lively spirit that always comforted her daughter. "We'll just have to keep trying, Amy."

Amy took a deep breath. "You're right. Let's go.

That night, Strength approached Hope, who stood near Bahar's crib. "How is she?"

Hope looked up. "She retreats more and more into herself."

Demonic laughter cackled down the hall outside the room. Hope knew the demons were preparing to attack.

"The dark one's forces are strong here," Strength said softly. "They must give you much strife at night."

Hope nodded.

Despair's lingering scent hung around Bahar like a disease. He and the demons under his command had attacked Hope and Bahar repeatedly over the past few months. Hope, who was a great warrior, had fought them off so far, but he could only fight so many alone.

"Tonight is the start of many things," Strength said. "The Lord has sent me to help you from now on."

"So it begins," said Hope, and he swung his sword at the approaching demons.

Chapter 22

One Year Later

Amy held Bahar and looked down at her blank, dark eyes, staring at the wall. She tried to blink back tears. *Lord, look at her! She used to talk and smile when she saw me. Now she just stares, or her eyes roll back. Her head is getting flat from lying in that crib all the time, her hands are twisting together, and she just rocks back and forth.* Tears fell onto Bahar's face, catching her eyelashes and making her blink absently. *God, why won't you just let us adopt her?*

Amy heard the squeak of wheels near the door. She turned and saw Yasmur, the translator, pushing Gulistan in her wheelchair. Gulistan was as smart as any older girl her age, but because she was physically handicapped, she was housed in this part of the orphanage.

Gulistan smiled at Amy, gesturing for Yasmur to bring her closer. With Yasmur translating, Gulistan said, "Thank you, again, Amy, for bringing my wheelchair."

Amy smiled and replied, "We can thank God, Gulistan. He led people to donate the wheelchairs for children here. You look very nice in it."

After Yasmur finished, Gulistan smiled again and nodded. Her eyes, large from malnourishment, looked at Bahar. "You want to take her home now?"

"Yes."

"She will be much better when she is with you in America."

Amy nodded.

"She spoke to me yesterday," Gulistan continued cheerfully. "When I feed her, I have to tell her, Eat! Eat! over and over again.

So yesterday, when I brought food for her, she whispered *Eeeeaaat* to me."

Amy laughed in relief. Bahar could still speak! "You do a good job feeding her, Gulistan. I am glad that God has put you in Bahar's life."

The compliment made Gulistan smile again. She had been feeding Bahar at least one meal a day for the last few months. "Did you see what Fatima bought with the money you pay me?" asked Gulistan.

"No, what did you get yourself this time?"

Gulistan held up her bony wrist. A shiny gold bracelet sparkled there. "Fatima says that the streets of heaven are paved with gold like this. Is it not beautiful?"

Amy replied. "Yes, it is beautiful. But not as beautiful as you, Gulistan."

"You make me laugh, Amy," Gulistan said with a grin, "but I'm glad that you like it. Don't be sad for Bahar. Jesus and the angels are with her, just like we pray for them to be. And you are working so hard to free her. She must be released."

Becky appeared at the door. She was breathing hard and she looked tired. "Amy, we're getting ready to start another feeding. Some of the team members are still uncomfortable with how to feed the children. Could you help them out?" She turned to Bahar. "Hey, sweetie," she cooed, and Bahar opened her eyes. "We'll get you out of here soon, won't we? You just sit tight. You're gonna make such a precious granddaughter, don't you know?" Becky looked at Amy. "Stay here with her. I can find someone else to help."

"Oh, no, Mom, I'll do it." Amy laid Bahar back in her crib. "Bahar will get plenty of loving when we bring her home. For now, I'm here to love on the rest of the kids too. Why are you breathing so hard?"

Becky shrugged. "I've just been really tired lately, I guess. There's so much going on. Maybe I need more sleep." Her eyes glistened as she looked from Amy to Bahar.

As they left the room, Gulistan watched Bahar's hand momentarily stretch toward Amy, and then fall limp.

❦

"Faith! Courage!" God called.

"We're here, Lord."

"A time has come when my faithful children will meet their greatest challenges in the story so far."

The angels bowed.

"What happens will stop Becky from returning to my children in the orphanage for a long time." The Lord's face was sad, but resolute. "The dark one will bring much pain, but Becky, Graham, and their family must endure this hardship in order to grow in their faith and ministry and trust in me more."

❦

Two months later, on the next trip, Becky carted a huge bottle of bath soap into the tiled bathroom. "All right, Derya, in here," she called.

When Yasmur repeated Becky's words, a young native woman came in with a pile of towels stacked so high only her eyes and dark hair poked over the top.

"You can set those down over there, Derya; then I can bring the kids in."

Four hours later, with help from Derya and Yasmur, Becky had finished bathing all forty children from one of the rooms. Derya and

Yasmur groaned as they got up from their knees and began to stretch their stiff joints.

"I can't believe we got them all done," said Derya. "That was amazing."

"It was," Yasmur agreed, and she and Derya began to pick up towels that had been flung across the floor by excited kids.

Becky was still on her knees. Her normally vibrant face had turned the color of the walls in the hallway.

"Becky! Are you all right?" Derya cried in Turkish.

"I can't get up," Becky gasped. "I can't . . . breathe."

Chapter 23

"When did you and your wife first suspect something was wrong?" asked the specialist, Dr. Robinson, at the Phoenix hospital. He pushed his glasses up and scanned the reports from Becky's doctor.

"I . . . I'm not sure," Graham answered. "She's been having a real hard time breathing for the past couple of months. But we just wrote it off due to stress and lack of sleep. But two weeks ago in Turkey, she could hardly breathe or move at all for a good number of minutes. Thankfully she made it back. But we need to get to the bottom of this. That's why we're here."

"She's had symptoms for a while, then. Any other symptoms?" asked the doctor, scribbling on the paper in his clipboard.

"Yes, for the past two years, she's always felt under the weather for a couple of days after she's flown."

"What do you mean 'under the weather'?"

"She said she's had headaches and dizziness and trouble breathing, as if the blood wasn't getting to her arms and legs fast enough for her to move. This last trip was the worst. I'm really worried."

Faith encouraged Graham, "They need this information to help Becky. Just keep answering the questions. . . . Be easy on them, Dr. Robinson; you know how worried he must be."

"And how many times have you flown since you started having symptoms?" Dr. Robinson asked Becky.

"Um . . ." Becky tried to mentally count her trips. "About twenty."

"Pardon?"

"About twenty."

Two more decisive scribbles on the paper. "That's quite a lot of trips. Does your work require you to travel a lot?"

"Kind of."

"All right," Dr. Robinson said decisively. "Mrs. Bates, if you will follow me, we can start running some tests. Let's see what we can do to get this figured out."

He strode across the office and disappeared behind swinging doors. Graham smiled half-heartedly and tried not to look too worried as his wife followed the specialist.

"They are having a hard time accepting your aid, aren't they?" said Compassion.

"Yes," said Faith. "We can whisper comfort to them, but they must choose to accept it. Sometimes their flesh—their own pain and fear—is stronger than any demon's work."

"Have confidence in your Lord, Graham," added Faith.

Sitting down on one of the hard chairs in the office, Graham clasped his hands absently and stared at the floor. *God, I know that you are in this situation somehow,* he prayed. *Please be with Becky. Please give her strength. And if it's in your will, heal her.* Graham felt comforted by the knowledge that God was watching and involved with whatever was happening in the hospital beyond the swinging doors.

Despair bowed before his dark lord. "You called for me, my master?"

"I have been watching your work," Satan hissed. *"Now that Becky is unable to come to the orphanage, my forces are stronger there than ever."*

"That nation and every orphanage in it will always be in your stronghold, my lord."

"Yes." Satan shrugged. *"For thousands of years, I have held that part of the world in my fist, and I will keep it there. You, my demon, have followed my orders well. Consider yourself pardoned."*

He waved Despair away and stared blankly at the wall, brooding for a long time. Surely after a blow like this, Graham and Becky and everyone involved with Least of These would regret ever going to the orphanage.

Mark and Amy watched their children carefully. The eight-year-old twins, Becca and Beth, kept exchanging glances with each other across the living room. Mark and Amy could tell that they were anxious and worried. Graham, at ten, was harder to read. He had stopped his video game and was looking first at Beth and Becca and then at his parents.

Mark could feel the children's apprehension like a cloud of thick, hot smoke. He took a deep breath and exhaled slowly. He couldn't avoid talking any longer; the kids had to know what was happening, and it was his job to tell them.

"Your grandma," he began, "is very sick." As he spoke, his voice became stronger, more assuring. "She has what are called blood clots, twenty-six of them, in her lungs and legs. It's like a blood disease; her blood isn't going where it needs to go in order for her to move around and talk like she's supposed to. She's staying at the hospital for a while."

Faith and Compassion watched the family silently.

"Is she gonna die?" Becca asked.

Mark saw that Amy wanted to smile but couldn't seem to find the energy. Leave it to Becca to ask what was on her mind. "We don't know," he answered. "This disease is very rare and hard to cure. What we can do is pray for her and Grandpa. This is really hard for both of them right now, and they need lots of help from Jesus and the angels."

Graham and Becca just looked at him. Beth nodded.

"Tomorrow after school, we'll all go to the hospital and see Grandpa. Maybe they'll even let us see Grandma for a little bit. If you guys made cards or letters or something, that would be very nice." Mark glanced at Amy, and she nodded reassuringly. "Do you all understand?" he asked.

"So Grandma's not going to die?"

"Honey, we're all gonna die someday," Mark said. "It's just a matter of when God wants us home with him."

"I'll make a card for her tonight," Beth said.

Graham didn't say anything.

Chapter 24

A month later, Adam Bates stood over Bahar's crib. His mother had been in and out of the hospital, and he had promised her he would lead as many Hug Team trips as he could. Adam had also promised Mark and Amy that he would check on Bahar and give her lots of attention. Like his sister, he had noticed that Bahar was looking sicker every time they saw her.

Now, as he lifted Bahar into his arms and cradled her, his dark Korean skin contrasted sharply with her pale flesh. Her hair, which had grown back since the last shave, stood up in thick, dirty clumps. Although Bahar was staring at the ceiling, Adam was sure he felt a wave of relief run through her as he rocked her back and forth.

"It's been a long time since my sister has seen you, hasn't it?" he said quietly. "They all send their love, even Graham, Beth, and Becca. They haven't met you yet, but you're gonna love having them as your brother and sisters."

Suddenly Bahar blinked and focused on Adam's face. He felt a thrill of excitement.

Hope and Strength smiled as they watched Bahar's interaction with Adam.

"They asked me to start calling you Emma," he said, "because that's what your name will be when you come home to live with them. What do you think of that, huh? What do you think of that, Emma?"

Bahar blinked at him again.

"You're gonna like it with Mark and Amy. They're great parents.

And if you think about it, Emma," Adam said, smiling, knowing that Bahar couldn't understand a word he was saying, "if you think about it, pray for your grandma, my mom, Becky. She's in the hospital and wants to see you when you come home to all of us."

Bahar sighed, and her eyes resumed their unfocused stare.

"Don't worry, Adam," said Hope. "Your prayers are heard."

When Graham walked into Becky's hospital room and sat down next to Becky's bed, she held out her hand, and he reached over and grasped it.

"How are you feeling?"

"Sick as a dog, but okay. You know I hate going in and out of these hospitals. I wish they could have taken care of these blood clots on my first stay. Have you talked to Dr. Robinson?"

"He said the tests went well and the results are being evaluated." Graham settled his gaze somewhere on the wall beside Becky. "He doesn't know what, if anything, he will be able to do."

Squeezing his hand, Becky sighed and leaned her head against her pillow. "Well, if he's meant to find anything that can help me, he will."

"He did say there is one thing he's sure of."

"Yes?"

"He said that all the flying back and forth made this condition a lot worse than it would have been."

Becky nodded. She understood what he was trying to say.

"Honey," Graham asked, "do you have any regrets about what we've done at the orphanage or with Least of These?"

Becky sighed again and looked away. "I can't help but wonder why I didn't find someone else to lead the Hug Teams more often. Or if I still would have done Least of These if I had known I would end up here." She turned and looked at her husband, tears in her eyes. "But, honey, God told us what we were to do in such a straightforward, positive way, and we have seen so much good come from it. I know that God has put hope and joy into those kids through our obedience to him. Even if I knew that I would die from this disease, I still would have gone and done what we've done."

Graham smiled and squeezed her hand. "That's my girl," he said.

Chapter 25

"*H*ow is the little one?" Grace asked Hope and Strength. The three angels watched Bahar lying listlessly in her crib.

"Not well," said Strength.

"The King has prevented any demons from poisoning her mind," Hope said, "but her physical body has been getting worse. She can no longer eat the food that the state workers give her, and what Adam and the Hug Team manage to get into her is not enough. And Bahar needs much more than food in order to survive. She is dying."

"Has the Lord said anything to you about whether she will survive?" Strength asked.

Grace shook his head. "None can fathom his plan."

"Wouldn't it be nice to know what was happening on at least one side?" said Despair, entering the room with the demons under his command. "Especially since your master is so secretive about his."

The angels said nothing, but their swords were drawn and blazing hungrily; a battle was certain.

"It's such a sad existence," Despair continued. "You are caught up like pawns in your master's story, just ordered to blindly follow his commands."

"Your deceptions won't work here," Hope said, grimacing..

The demons began to spread out, forming a circle around the angels and Bahar's crib.

"You have no idea what's going on!" Despair spat. "Admit it! What kind of 'lord of lords' keeps his servants blinded?"

Strength smiled, gripping his sword tighter as the circle began to close in on him and his companions. "Any lord," he said, "is entitled to keep to himself what he believes should be kept secret. That is what separates him

*from his subjects. And even if we do not know what is going to happen,
our Lord does."*

*Simultaneously, the demons gave a piercing shriek and pounced
upon the three angels.*

❧

"Hi Mom!" Beth called as she, Becca, and Graham walked into
the house and began to pile their backpacks by the door. There was
no answer, and the house was unusually quiet

"Mom?" Graham called. He looked in the kitchen. "Not here,"
he called to the twins.

"Maybe she went to the store," Becca suggested.

"She would've left a note or something," Graham said.

"Let's check her room," Beth said. She led the way upstairs and
down the hall. Her parents' bedroom door was closed, and she put
her ear to the door. "She's on the phone," she said. "It sounds bad,
like she's about to cry. You know, when her voice starts to shake."

Graham didn't say anything, but his face grew serious.

"Let me listen," Becca said, and Beth moved over. "Is it about
Grandma?" she whispered.

Beth nodded. "She must be getting worse."

❧

"Courage," the Lord said, "it is time."

The angel bowed low before the throne.

*The Lord continued, "Becky has proven herself strong and faithful,
and she has not cursed me in anything that Satan has thrown in her
path. It is time for her to be rewarded."*

"Yes, Lord."

Courage and the group of angels around him scanned the hospital room. Wires and tubes crisscrossed the floor like a giant spiderweb, and the steady beep of the heart monitor seemed to echo in the apparent peacefulness.

"He's here," Courage whispered to his companions, and they spread out through the room, hands ready to draw their swords. Becky's sleeping form was visible in the bed in the middle of the room. Quietly, stealthily, the angels waited.

"He will reveal himself," Courage said.

Suddenly, the heart monitor began to beep erratically. The angels' swords roared to life, and a deep, venomous laugh rose above the sound of the monitor.

Two nurses rushed into Becky's room.

"We're losing her!" one of them cried. "Code blue!"

"You came to defeat me, angels?" Suffering asked, his twisted form appearing in front of Courage.

Courage's sword was pointed toward Suffering, "Your time here is over."

With that, the angel attacked. Suffering ducked and then howled as the sword dug into his arm. The demon lunged toward the angel, swinging his own sword.

"Demons, to me!" he shouted. The next instant, half a dozen fallen ones appeared in the room and began to hack at the angels. Suffering used their sudden appearance to duck out of sight. Courage's eyes darted through the celestials, searching for the lost demon. Around him, angels and demons grappled, ducked, and hurled themselves against each other,

all amid the delicate instruments that surrounded Becky. Suddenly, Courage caught a flash of Suffering's gnarled head, sliding behind Justice and Pain; then, as Justice blocked Pain's sword, Suffering plunged his own weapon into Justice's back. The angel gasped in surprise, and the demons let out a howl of victory.

Courage darted across the room and grabbed the demon with one hand, throwing him back to where they had been battling before. Suffering scrambled to his feet, his eyes wide with fear. He searched for his weapon, but it lay at Courage's feet.

Courage strode across the room, "It's over, demon," he said steadily.

Suffering whined piteously, and the next moment, the battle was finished.

The demons vanished from the room. Courage went to Becky's side. He watched the doctor checking Becky, his face tight with worry. Courage could barely hear the sound of her shallow, labored breath. He sheathed his sword and then touched a glowing hand to her face. At first, her flesh felt cold and looked deathly pale compared to his golden tones. But Courage's touch seemed to warm Becky and fill her lungs with new air.

He whispered, "Rest easy, Becky. The Lord is healing you." He nodded to two of his companions, and they posted themselves on either side of Becky's bed. They would stay with her for the remainder of her time in the hospital. With that, Courage and the rest of the company disappeared.

Becky woke up to bright light all around her. She lifted a hand to rub her eyes, expecting to feel the cord of the IV pull on her arm. Instead, she was surprised to feel her arm free and unrestrained. She sat up and looked around just as a nurse walked into the room.

"Good morning, Mrs. Bates!" said the nurse. "I hear that you're feeling much better this morning."

"Good morning, Paige," Becky answered without thinking; then she said slowly, "I *am* feeling much better, now that you mention it."

"I'm glad." Paige smiled and began to check Becky's vitals. "Dr. Robinson will be here in a moment. He was so worried about you last night, and when we called and told him that you had pulled through it, he was happier than we've heard him in a long time."

"What happened last night?" Becky asked. "I don't remember."

"Oh, Mrs. Bates, we were so concerned about you. Your blood pressure dropped to 60 over 40; your heart rate was up to the 130s and was in V-fib. We thought it was almost over; and then the next thing we knew, your vitals stabilized and you were on your way to coming back to us."

Becky nodded and smiled. "Well, I'm not sure what V-fib is, but I like the good news!" she said cheerfully. Her eyes had begun to regain their sparkle.

"I'd call it a miracle," Dr. Robinson said as he entered the room. "How are you feeling, Becky?"

"Great," Becky answered. "A little weak, but great."

"You'll feel weak for a while," Dr. Robinson said with a nod, sitting down on the swivel chair and pulling out a clipboard. He pushed up his glasses. "You might regress a little bit, so we'll have to keep you here for a few days. But I think you've made it through the worst, Mrs. Bates."

Becky nodded. "Does Graham know?" she asked.

Dr. Robinson smiled. "He's on the way now, and the rest of your family will be here later today."

A week later, Becky was back at home, taking medicine and trying to keep her schedule as easy as possible. Dr. Robinson had forbidden her from doing too much work until he was sure she was really stabilized. His definition of "too much work" included any Hug Team trips. Although it was hard to face, Becky resigned herself to simply coordinating trips from her home and letting Adam, Amy, and the other long-time Least of These volunteers do the flying.

One day, as she was working on a budget for installing a new water heater in the handicapped building, Becky received a phone call.

"Becky? This is Tara. I have great news."

Chapter 26

"*A my!*"

Amy held the receiver away from her ear. Her mother was shouting over the phone. "Oh, honey, you won't believe what I've just found out! Tara just called. You know that Turkey has been going through some political changes, and one of the changes is . . ." Her voice trailed off as she caught her breath.

"Tell me, Mom," Amy prompted. Her heart was beating faster.

Becky laughed. "I can hardly believe it myself, but Tara said that the Turkish government has now made it legal for foreigners to adopt children there!"

"*What?*"

"I'm serious!"

"*Oh, my goodness!* That's wonderful!" Amy was laughing and jumping up and down. "Mom, are you absolutely serious?"

"Of course I am! Let's celebrate tonight and talk face-to-face when Graham and Mark get home."

Amy leaned against the counter. "All right, sounds good. I've got to call Mark right now!" She set the phone down and sank into a chair. She felt giddy. It was legal for her and Mark to adopt Bahar! They could bring her home!

"Hope, I have seen your faithfulness to the task I laid before you," said the Lord. *"You have worked tirelessly; never have you fallen when Satan's servants tried to defeat you. Now that Bahar's*

country has allowed me to change their constitution concerning
foreign adoption, your task must enter a new phase. And this one
will be even harder.

"My Spirit will be with you and Strength more than ever," He
continued. "It will need to be so, because Satan will continue to fight
against us. He will oppress you on all sides, but you will not be shaken.
And through his opposition, even more people will learn of my grace and
love through Christ's blood."

Hope looked up at the Lord's face. Its brilliance seemed to seep into
his being, energizing him.

"Go, Hope, and bring glory to my name."

Hope bowed and disappeared.

Beth stared up at her bedroom ceiling. After hearing her parents
tell her, Becca, and Graham that they were finally going to be able
to adopt Bahar, her mind was so full that she was having trouble
getting to sleep. She rolled over to face the wall, but she could still see
the light from Becca's lamp shining in the corner of her eye. Finally
she sat up. "What do you think of this whole thing?" she asked her
twin.

"You mean about Bahar?"

"Yeah."

Becca kept her eyes on her hands as she continued painting her
fingernails. "Umm, I don't know," she said. "It sounds neat. Uncle
Adam and Aunt Abby and Uncle Aaron are adopted, and I think
that's cool."

"Yeah," Beth sighed. "It'll be cool to have another sister."

"Yeah."

"How long do you think it'll take to get her here?" Beth asked.

Becca shrugged and screwed the top back onto the bottle of nail polish. "Mom and Grandma said that Mom could go over next month. So maybe a little while after that."

"Like a week, maybe? It's gonna be so interesting."

Becca waved her hands, trying to dry her fingernails. "Remember how they said Bahar might be mentally handicapped. What's that?" Becca asked.

"You know, like Emily's sister. She's really older than Emily, but her brain makes her act like she's two years old."

"Is that how Bahar's gonna be?"

Beth shrugged. "I guess so. Only she's a lot younger than us. I think they said, like, four or five or something. But I don't think they know for sure."

"Do Mom and Dad know how to take care of a mentally handicapped kid?"

"I don't know," Beth answered.

"Your parents are following God," Faith whispered to the sisters, "and he will equip them accordingly."

Becca shrugged. "But I guess it can't be too different. And it'll be cool having a sister who's always, like, four or five."

"We don't know if she'll always be like that, Becca," Beth said with a yawn. "Are you done yet?"

Becca felt her nails and then pulled up her blanket. "Yeah, I am." She turned out the light. But the darkness didn't quiet either girl's thoughts.

Chapter 27

"My lord, Amy and her friend Ruth are on their way to the orphanage now," Impatience hissed as he bowed low in front of the dark throne. "We have tried to stop them, but your enemy's spirit prevents us from getting too close. They hope to adopt the girl quickly." He felt a chill run through him as he glanced up at his master's face, and he looked down again. "However, we do know that after they land, they plan to meet with that Tara woman and the translator—"

"And from there they will go to Social Services to try to get the girl," the evil one interrupted moodily. "Chaos is following them, I assume?"

"As you commanded, my master."

There was a long silence. "And Prejudice and Shame are planting my seeds among Social Services," Satan eventually hissed. "Heeehhhh . . . I will call back Despair, Pain, and Suffering, and they will resume their work in the orphanage. They will know to do a better job this time than they did before. Meanwhile, Doubt and Anger will join them, along with the others." He clapped to summon Fear and Confusion.

Satan's sudden summons made Impatience jump. When the two demons appeared and saw their lord's face, they exchanged nervous glances with Impatience.

"You three listen carefully," Satan hissed. He was breathing harder, and one claw clenched and unclenched compulsively. "You will join Chaos as he follows the women. Torment them whenever you get a chance. My enemy may have surprised me by changing the constitution, but we will win in the end."

Something in the dark one's voice sent a thrill of excitement through Impatience; their lord had a plan!

"My enemy believes that rescuing this precious Bahar will bring him glory," Satan continued, *"but he will never get her. My enemy's absurd affection for his humans makes his next moves predictable."* Satan smiled. *"In this story, I will receive the glory in the end. All will see."* The dark one waved away Impatience and his companions. *"Now go. You know what you must do."*

<p>

Tara and Yasmur met Amy and Ruth at the airport and drove them to the hotel where the Hug Teams always stayed. Amy was grateful for the warm reception by the hotel staff, who remembered her.

Chaos, Impatience, Fear, and Confusion followed the two women to their room.

Amy noticed Ruth kept glancing at her as they unpacked their bags.

"What are you thinking, Amy?" Ruth finally asked. "You've been unusually quiet all evening."

"I don't know. Mark and I have known ever since we met Bahar that we had to adopt her. It never seemed like such a big deal, just obedience to God's command. . . . But the whole way over here, I've been wondering what in the world God is doing." She flopped her makeup bag onto the small bathroom counter.

Blocking the demons from getting too close to the women were four angels. Fear scowled at the celestials as they brandished their blades. He only needed to whisper a few key thoughts into Amy's heart. She shouldn't be worried about obedience; she should be worried about her family's happiness. Didn't she realize that Bahar would disrupt everything?

"Mark and I never planned to have another child; we were totally content with Graham and the girls. Mom and Dad adopted all of my siblings, of course, but I never really considered adoption for us."

Fear laughed as he heard Amy's words "There's nothing for me to do here after all, angels. Amy is already full of questions. She will grow discouraged with or without our help."

Confusion spoke up. "How can you angels of light just stand there and let Amy do this? You know that Bahar won't fit in with her family. Think of her children; what will their friends say? You're not doing any justice by stopping us from telling her the truth."

"Your lies don't fool us," Grace said quietly. "Our job is to obey the Lord. We don't always need to understand his ways. And Amy's questions are honest; her heart wants to glorify the Lord. There is nothing wrong with that."

Justice lifted his sword, but Grace stopped him. "This is not the time to initiate a battle. Remember that their father is the father of lies."

Opening the curtains, Amy gazed at the city around the hotel. The sun had just set, leaving a pale pink outline along the edges of the buildings on the horizon. "I guess my question is, why us? Why Bahar? What is it about this little girl that God would do all of this work and bring us here? And what is it about us that made God decide that we would be Bahar's family? . . . Maybe I'm overanalyzing."

"I don't think so," Ruth said. "You're just being honest. The reality is that we can't possibly know exactly what God's plan is in all of this, but he will work this out exactly the way he wants. Can we ask for anything more?"

"You're right," Amy agreed. "He must have a bigger plan than Mark and I do."

Grace smiled.

Chapter 28

Beth tried to do her homework. The house seemed so strange without Mom. Amy had only been gone for a day, but already the rooms seemed to echo in a sad, dusty way.

"Dad, how long will Mom be gone?" Becca called to Mark in the kitchen.

"Sis, you've asked that a million times today." Graham looked up from his video game.

"This trip feels different," Beth said. "We always knew exactly when Mom was coming back before, and it was never more than two weeks."

"We don't know for sure, honey," Mark answered from the kitchen. "At least a few weeks. That's normal for adopting a child from another country."

Becca twirled her pencil and sighed. Beth looked back down at her homework. "She'd better not stay for a month," she said softly.

"What?" said Becca.

"Never mind. Just thinking," Beth replied. What had Mom told them before she left? *Whenever you miss me or start thinking scared thoughts, pray.* Closing her eyes, she prayed silently.

Amy was nervous the next day as Tara drove her and Ruth, along with Yasmur, to the Office of Social Services to discover what adopting Bahar would entail.

"Listen, Amy," Tara said as she drove, "there's something I want to tell you, and it may be hard to digest. You know that foreign adoption has never occurred, as far as we know, here in Turkey—especially not the adoption of a handicapped child."

"That's what we've been hearing since we first looked into adopting Emma."

"The thing is, Amy, that although the constitution says foreign adoption is now legal, no one here has ever done it before. We can't assume that they thought out an adoption process before they agreed to make adoption legal."

"I understand, Tara. Mark and I have talked about that."

"And you know that this culture doesn't promote caring for handicapped children. Social Services will be extremely suspicious of you wanting to adopt Bahar."

"Suspicious of her helping a helpless child?" Ruth asked.

The other three women nodded. "That's just a reality here, Ruth," Tara explained. "This is a Muslim culture. And although Islam is family oriented, that family loyalty stops when it comes to children with disabilities."

"Why would that make a difference?" Ruth asked.

Tara turned the van down a narrow road. The buildings on either side, hundreds of years old, stared down at the four women and blocked out the sun. "Islam teaches that those children are cursed, unclean, and no one wants to be a part of something that Allah has cursed."

"That seems so cruel."

Yasmur picked up the explanation. "It is cruel from a Christian point of view, but it makes sense to those who live in this culture. It provides a way, however, for us to really show God's unconditional love. Just look at how God has used Least of These to proclaim his love not only to the orphans but also to the orphanage workers, to Ahmed and his family, to the people who came on the Hug Teams—to me, even, and I'm just the translator."

"And that's just like God," Tara said, parking the van. "He takes the bad parts of a culture and uses them to reflect his glory."

"Good point," Ruth said. "Let's pray that God does that here, for Mark and Amy. I'm worried about this meeting."

They walked toward the front doors of the prestigious-looking Social Services building, and Amy grabbed Ruth's hand. "Ruth, I feel like I'm going to be sick."

Ruth squeezed Amy's hand. "It'll be okay. God is in control. Remember, He's big enough to be in Social Services."

"He is, Amy." Grace smiled as he, Justice, Compassion, and Faith surrounded the women.

Amy nodded and took a deep breath.

"All right, ladies," Tara said. "Remember what I told you in the van. This is the first time this country has even considered foreign adoption, so don't expect to walk out of here today with the custody papers. Yasmur, I'll let you do all of the translating, and Ruth, you're our prayer warrior. Okay, everybody ready?"

All three nodded.

"Amy," Tara said quietly as they walked up the steps, "Remember, God's timing may not be our timing." She laughed. "I think I'm almost as anxious as you are. But, the fact that we've gotten this far in the adoption process is a miracle." She opened the door and they filed in.

Chapter 29

"Hmm, so it didn't go so well?" Becky asked over the phone that evening. "Well, we were expecting something like that."

"But did she get Emma?" Beth asked impatiently.

"Grandma . . ." Becca pleaded.

Becky glanced at them and slowly shook her head.

"Did Tara tell them the constitution now says that adopting Emma is legal?" Becky asked. ". . . So you just have to wait while they investigate, and then they will call you? . . . Well, honey, I love you."

"Tell Mom that I love her too!" Beth said.

"Me too!" Becca echoed.

"Can we talk to her?" asked Graham, looking up from his homework.

Becky offered the phone to Mark.

"Soon as I'm done talking to your mom, you can all have a turn," he said.

"Can I talk to her first?" Graham asked.

Becky offered hugs to Beth and Becca. They slipped out of her arms quickly, anxious to talk to their mom. It didn't sound like Amy would be coming home anytime soon.

Grace, Justice, Faith, and Compassion bowed before the throne. "Lord, when we arrived at Social Services, the dark one's servants were waiting for us, as you said they would be," Grace began, "and they whispered words of prejudice and shame."

"We encouraged the four women," Justice continued, "and then Chaos and his companions appeared."

emma's STORY   111

"I saw you fighting them," the Lord said.

The angels exchanged glances. "We did when they attacked us, but we did not defeat them," said Grace.

"When they realized that we weren't trying to defeat them," Faith added, *"they stopped fighting and began to feed as many lies to the humans as they could."*

"The women became discouraged, but Grace and Faith comforted them, and their faith in you was strong enough to defeat the demons for now," said Compassion.

The Lord nodded at his angels with approval. "It is good that you did not destroy the demons. Their lies and their place in Social Services have an important part in revealing my glory."

"It could have been worse," Ruth commented cheerfully the next afternoon. "Honestly, at least they didn't throw us out of the building for requesting something so ridiculous."

Ahmed grinned at Ruth's words as he maneuvered through traffic.

"They almost did," Amy said. "You'd think we had just suggested that everyone in Social Services should jump off a cliff. But you're right, Ruth, we weren't expecting a red carpet, and we certainly didn't get one. At least the whole adoption process is started."

"And that's the key," Yasmur said. "Now that it's started, we just have to keep on going."

"Here we are," Ahmed said, pulling the van into the parking lot in front of the orphanage. "I return at four o'clock. If you need anything, call me. It was nice to meet you, Ruth; I hope you have a pleasant stay."

"Thank you, Ahmed," said the women as they climbed out of the van and headed into the orphanage.

Chaos, Impatience, Fear, and Confusion slunk after them.

The Hope Room came alive when the women entered.

"And this is Levent," Amy said, hugging the boy in front of her and Ruth. "Levent, you've grown so much since the last time I was here! You're a young man now." Pointing to Levent, Amy said the Turkish word for *grow*.

Levent smiled and stood a little straighter.

"Levent, this is my friend Ruth." Amy put her hand on Ruth's arm. "Ruth," she said. "She's a friend." Amy repeated the native word for *friend*. Levent's smile got big as he peered at Ruth through his one good eye and gave her a big hug.

"It's nice to meet you, Levent!" Ruth laughed.

"He was one of Mom and Dad's first miracles," Amy explained. "We've always had a special place for him in our hearts."

Suddenly, Levent saw Yasmur walk through the door, and he hurried away to greet her. Ruth watched Levent hobble toward Yasmur and give her a loving, clumsy hug.

"He's repulsive," Fear whispered to Ruth. "Did you see his milky white blind eye and missing teeth? How could a kid like that hold a special place with anyone?" Fear felt a tap on his shoulder and turned to meet Compassion's steely gaze.

"Don't even go there, demon." Compassion's voice was like ice.

One girl straightened up and squealed, "Ma-ma-ma-ma-mah! Ma-ma-ma-ma-mah!"

"Hello, Mamike!" Amy cooed, grasping her scrawny hand. "You're hungry, aren't you? Fatima will be here in a moment to feed you."

"Fatima?" Ruth asked.

"She's in charge of the full-time workers here whom Least of These has hired to keep the kids fed, keep diapers changed, give baths, things like that."

Ruth looked puzzled. "But don't the state workers do that?"

Amy gave a rueful smile. "You'd think so, wouldn't you?"

Amy shouted over the ruckus, "Here's Fatima now!"

After exchanging introductions, Amy asked Fatima how Bahar was.

Fatima shrugged, but her face was still glowing, "She is not as good as she could be if she were with you," she said while Yasmur translated, "but she has as much care as we can give her and all of the children." Her face grew serious. "Amy, did you hear about Gulistan?"

Amy looked up, puzzled, "No, I didn't."

Fatima picked up a child who was tugging at her sleeve, then sighed, not meeting Amy's eyes. "She died last week."

Amy stared at Fatima for a few seconds, not comprehending what Fatima had said. *Gulistan . . . dead?* She found a chair and sat down. Gulistan had seemed so much healthier, so much more alive than most of the children at the orphanage.

"How did she die?" Amy asked.

"She got sick and refused to take the medicine that we offered her. She said that she would rather be with Jesus than stay here any longer." Fatima's face was sad. "Don't worry, Amy. We must not be sorrowful for those who are in Christ, as the Word says. Instead, let us move on to those still living. Would you like to see Emma?"

Amy nodded and followed Fatima numbly. Gulistan was dead,

like so many of the other orphans she and her parents had known. She hoped God would allow her to adopt Bahar before Bahar too had joined their numbers.

Fatima led Amy and Ruth to Bahar's crib, and Amy caught her breath. The little girl looked like a baby doll as she slept silently on the hard mattress. She was thinner than Amy had ever seen her, and her skin was almost translucent in its paleness.

"Have strength, Amy," Hope whispered.

"Hello, Emma," Amy whispered softly. Gently, she traced the little girl's cheek with her finger. Bahar's eyes instantly opened. As the girl and the woman locked gazes, Bahar's mouth twisted into a small smile.

"She recognizes you," Fatima said with satisfaction.

Amy didn't reply. Lifting Bahar into her arms, she cradled her gently. The girl was so light.

"We have been trying to hold her and feed her every chance we get," Fatima said through Yasmur. "She still refuses food much of the time, but she responds well to the holding."

"You do a good work, Fatima. I'm glad that you are here."

Ruth watched in awe.

"But all of Fatima's good work won't stop my lord's work," Chaos hissed.

The angels exchanged looks.

Chapter 30

After a week of waiting for a phone call, Amy returned to Social Services unannounced, with Ruth and Yasmur.

"Greetings, greetings," said a large, older woman in the office to which they were escorted. Her dark eyes darted back and forth between the three women. "My secretary just told me that you have been waiting to hear from us. Sit here, dear," she said, and pointed for Amy to sit in one of the plush chairs as Yasmur translated.

"Please forgive us for our rudeness," the woman continued. "We never meant to make you come looking for us. Let me introduce myself. My name is Alara Basar. I am the head of Social Services, and I will answer any questions you have about the social services in our country."

Amy cleared her throat. "Well, ma'am, my name is Amy Sneed, these are my friends, and I am interested in adopting a young handicapped girl in the orphanage."

While Yasmur translated, Amy observed a slight change in Alara's expression. Her features never moved, but the light in her eyes seemed to darken.

"Why would a wealthy American want to adopt one of the cursed?" Shame whispered to Alara. "Of course, the children aren't as well cared for in the orphanage as they would be in someone's home, but that isn't this woman's responsibility. This infidel thinks she is better than you; she thinks that her compassion is greater than your country's."

"Well, what you suggest is perfectly legal under our new constitution," Alara said when Yasmur finished. "However, you may not know this, but we have never handled any form of foreign adoption before."

"But you did make provision for it in the constitution," Amy said.

"Of course. But you see, we don't have any process that you can follow. We have no papers, no forms, no procedures, nothing right now. We're not sure when we will have any. It could take months. Who knows?" She shrugged. "The best thing for you to do is to go home, and when we have the right papers ready, we will contact you." Alara glanced at Amy and nodded, waiting for Yasmur to finish translating.

That sounds familiar, Amy thought. *Go home and we'll contact you . . .*

Yasmur looked at Amy, waiting for a reply.

Lord, she prayed, *Mrs. Basar just wants me to go home so they won't have to deal with me anymore. This whole situation is yours; what do you want me to do?* She had learned, from watching Tara and her mother work in the orphanage, never to back down. But she wondered where the line was. Amy looked at Mrs. Basar. "Going home isn't an option. We have to do everything that we can."

Yasmur nodded and smiled.

"But tell her that in a nicer way," Amy suggested before Yasmur began to translate.

Mrs. Basar nodded solemnly as Yasmur spoke. She looked frustrated, but she kept smiling. "Mrs. Sneed, what you are asking is impossible."

Yasmur turned to Amy and translated the reply wearily.

Amy nodded and said, "Yes, I got that impression!" *Lord, by the end of this conversation, I'm not going to need a translator.* "It must be possible," Amy replied. "Your constitution clearly allows it."

Chaos whispered to Amy, "The constitution may allow it, but our lord is stronger than this human government."

Justice eyed the demon darkly.

"Of course, our constitution allows it," Mrs. Basar agreed, speaking slowly.

"Then what is the problem?" asked Amy. *Just say you'll at least try to work this out.*

Amy saw Mrs. Basar's eyes widen a little bit as she shuffled some papers needlessly. She was running out of excuses.

Shame whispered to Mrs. Basar, "Look at this woman, with her nicely done hair and her fine clothes. She thinks she's better than you. She's just waiting for you to serve her the way she wants everyone else to serve her. Life doesn't revolve around her. So why should you go through the headaches of giving the child to her? You don't know anything about this woman. What is her family really like? Does she have a good marriage? Does she beat her kids?"

"We don't have a program or application that can help us find out more about you and your family," Mrs. Basar said, her mind racing. "We have to keep the welfare of the children as our highest priority, and without more knowledge of your family, we cannot know for sure that the child you want to adopt will be well cared for."

Amy was shocked. The children's welfare wasn't even a low priority at the orphanage. Why did it matter now? *Lord, what do I say to that? I don't want to offend her, but these arguments are ridiculous.*

"Remember who you represent, Amy," Grace whispered. "You and your friends may be the only interaction Mrs. Basar ever has with

Christians. This story is not just about you adopting Bahar. It is about revealing the glory of the Father everywhere."

Amy took a deep breath. "I understand your concern, Mrs. Basar, and I am willing to work this out with you. I can give you information about me and my family, answer any questions you want. I will do everything I can to get this child."

"Listen to this woman!" Prejudice hissed angrily. "She thinks you and your country are inadequate in the care of these children! But who is she to think she can fly across the ocean and start pulling children away from you?"

The coldness in Mrs. Basar's eyes increased.

Chaos laughed and said to the watching angels, "My master's hold is stronger here than you think. Your lord might have power in the orphanage, but Social Services is my lord's domain."
The angels remained silent and watched as Mrs. Basar began to speak again.

"I know where you come from. You Americans are all the same. What makes you believe that you can tell us here in Turkey what to do and what is right for these children?" Mrs. Basar's voice became like ice. "You're younger than I am, you're richer than I am, you're prettier than I am, and I'm going to make your life hell and do everything I can to stop you!" The venom in Mrs. Basar's words caught Yasmur off guard.

"Go ahead, Yasmur, translate that for her, word for word," Mrs. Basar demanded. "And then, leave."

Chapter 31

The next day, Ben and Tara dropped Ruth off at the airport to fly home and then took Amy to find an attorney to help with the adoption. The law office looked much like the orphanage, with peeling paint and crumbling walls.

Mr. Muhammed immediately leaped at the opportunity to represent Amy.

"Of course," he said, nodding enthusiastically after Ben explained the situation to him. "Mrs. Sneed's case is perfectly valid, and I will do all I can to get that little boy to her." He extended his hand.

"Little girl," Ben corrected.

"The fools," Chaos snickered.

"Of course," Mr. Muhammed smiled. "Mrs. Sneed, I must tell you, we have never worked with foreign adoption here before, as far as I know, so there is no telling how long it will take. You could be here for a month at least before you can take Balar home."

"Bahar," Ben corrected again, before he translated for Amy. "Do we want to trust him after he's made all these mistakes?" he added, half joking.

"He's only human," Tara reasoned. "I would still trust him. But that's really your call, Amy."

God, only you know what this Mr. Muhammed is going to do. Mark and I are going to be paying him to help us get our daughter. What do you think? Presently, Amy took a deep breath. "Let's go for it."

In the darkness surrounding the throne, the evil one wheezed, "Report, my demon."

Chaos bowed. "Amy and the Nelsons were led to the lawyer who will work in our favor. Through him, you will drag them backwards."

Satan remained silent for a few moments. Chaos glanced up at him anxiously, trying to read what was going on in the evil one's thoughts. Was he satisfied with the demons' obedience? Was he angry with something that Chaos had forgotten? The demon remembered what had happened to Despair when he had failed.

"I know that you do well, Chaos," Satan said. "And I will monitor your continued work throughout this battle. Do not fail me."

Chaos bowed. "My lord, we have stopped them from progressing quickly."

"Progressing quickly?" Satan hissed. "They must be stopped from progressing at all!"

C:~

"Hey, Graham! How long has your mom been gone?" Kevin and Graham and four other boys walked out of the gas station toward their bikes.

Graham shrugged. "I don't know. Two weeks, maybe." He opened the bottled water he had bought in the gas station and gulped some down.

"Where is she?" Jason asked. He was a big kid with curly, fiery red hair. Sometimes he could be a bully.

"She's in the Middle East, adopting a kid," Kevin answered for Graham.

"Whoa, adopting a kid? That's cool . . . I guess. But why?"

Graham shrugged and picked up his bike. "My grandparents do mission trips and stuff for this handicapped orphanage, and my parents felt like they needed to adopt one of the kids there."

"Whoa," Jason said. "You didn't tell us they're adopting a *handi-capped* kid. So what, is it gonna be in a wheelchair or something?"

Graham sighed. He had been avoiding a conversation like this ever since his mom left.

"Honestly, I don't know," he answered, and he flicked up the kickstand of his bike and began to pedal down the sidewalk. He didn't know what he thought about any of it, and he tried to picture having a sister in a wheelchair. The idea was kind of weird, but not too weird to be possible. *I guess a sister is a sister whether she's in a wheelchair or not.*

A couple of the boys had sped ahead of him and were getting further away. Graham pumped the pedals harder to catch up with them.

Doubt whispered quietly, "Wheelchair or not, her brain will still be handicapped."

Graham passed under a spray of water from a sprinkler that was watering the road and sidewalk more than the yard it was in. Mom and Dad had asked him what he thought of having a mentally handicapped sister, and he wasn't sure. Part of him thought it would be fine, but another part kept gnawing at him with questions. He pedaled a little harder, trying to get his mind off it. But the questions were chewing holes in his faith in his parents' decision to adopt. He shook his head. *Will she sound weird when she talks? Will she drool? Will I have to change her diapers?*

Chapter 32

Tara stared at Mrs. Basar, who was sitting at her desk, arms crossed in front of her, smirking. A file labeled Foreign Adoption 000001 lay open on the desk next to the application that Amy and Tara had brought here a week ago. Mr. Muhammed was also staring at Mrs. Basar incredulously.

"Tara, what did she say?'" Amy asked.

"She asked if you plan on selling Emma or killing her."

It was Amy's turn to stare at Mrs. Basar. "Neither," she said calmly. "I want to adopt her as my daughter, not as merchandise."

Tara nodded and translated.

Mrs. Basar's face fell, and her eyes narrowed.

"She wants to know why you want to adopt one of the cursed children instead of a normal child."

Amy breathed deeply, praying for patience. "Tara, she asked me that last week, and the same exact question is in the application that's in front of her."

Tara forced herself to smile. "I think she knows that; she's just trying to waste time. She's trying to frustrate you out of continuing this battle. I've seen this tactic before."

"It won't work," Faith whispered. *"Have courage, Amy."*

Amy sighed. "I don't know what to say anymore. Mr. Muhammed, can you please take it from here?"

Tara quietly translated Amy's request while Mrs. Basar continued to watch Amy shrewdly.

Mr. Muhammed looked uneasy, and he stammered out a few

hesitant sentences with Mrs. Basar. Amy didn't like the look on Tara's face as she listened to the conversation.

"The battle is out of your hands, woman," Shame smirked, "and this pitiful lawyer you hired will only prolong your defeat."

Chaos hissed to the angels surrounding Amy. "You see? Your master's work is being destroyed by a lazy woman and a weak man. Is there anything more pitiful?"

"Now!" Justice shouted.

The four angels drew their swords out and leaped toward the demons, who howled and grasped their own weapons.

Tara tried to protest something Mrs. Basar and Mr. Muhammed said, but they ignored her.

The demons hacked wildly, at first outnumbering the angels by two. Suddenly, Chaos gave a wild yell, and more demons poured into the battle.

Soon, there weren't any angels left in the room. Dancing about, the demons howled in triumph.

Mrs. Basar and Mr. Muhammed finished speaking and shook hands.

"What just happened?" Amy asked.

Tara clenched her teeth. "I'll tell you on the way to my house. For now, the meeting just ended and we need to leave."

Amy and Tara shook hands with Mrs. Basar and followed Mr. Muhammed out of the building.

Leaning over the crib, Hope watched Bahar's face carefully. For the first time in months, her eyes were focusing on the room around her even when Amy was not around. The cracked fluorescent lights had been turned off, and night wrapped the room in shadowy darkness. Bahar turned her face to peer at the room through the bars of her crib.

"She is growing stronger now that Amy is visiting her and giving her personal care every day," Strength observed.

Hope nodded. "The Sneeds' prayers are strengthening her as well."

"She is getting stronger, is she?" an oily voice hissed.

The angels kept their faces calm, strong, chiseled features in place, as Despair appeared in the room, flanked by other demons. "We just keep running into each other, don't we?" he taunted. "Although, I guess that could be avoided if you two would stop invading my lord's territory."

The angels didn't reply.

Despair drew his sword and cackled, peering at Hope and Strength through the writhing blade. "I'm not going to waste my time with words," he said. "You know what my master wants."

The angels and the rest of the demons all drew their weapons, and Hope whirled when he heard a low laugh come from behind them, on the other side of Bahar's crib. Another crowd of demons had gathered there.

"You're outnumbered, angels," Despair commented coldly.

Hope and Strength smiled as their eyes lit up and their swords roared to life with heavenly fire. "You know better than that," Hope said.

"Holy is the Lord," said Strength.

"Okay, we need to rethink our choice of lawyer," Tara said over dinner that evening.

"I agree," Amy said. "I don't feel like we've made any progress through Mr. Muhammed."

"If anything, he's pulled us away from progress," Tara said.

"Fill me in," said Ben. "What happened today?"

"Absolutely nothing. He just sat there and scheduled another meeting."

"Which is exactly what he's done the past two weeks," Amy added. "Yasmur and I have met with several people from Social Services, and every time the conversation starts getting tense—as if they may decide something—he schedules another meeting. Do you think I should find another attorney?"

Ben nodded. "Let me talk to some people from church. Maybe they'll know someone."

"Good, I'm glad that's settled," Amy said. Maybe with a new lawyer, she could finish up the adoption and head back home soon. She was getting anxious to go home.

"My lord," Despair said with a bow. "You called for me?"

"Yes," Satan said with venom. "I want to know why you did not fulfill your orders concerning the little girl."

Despair suddenly felt icy cold. "We did what you ordered, my lord. We tried to kill her," he stammered. "But the girl's protection is too strong."

"So you could not defeat two simple angels?"

"There is much more than just the angels protecting Bahar, my lord," the demon answered awkwardly.

Satan snarled and sat back, thinking. "There is a way," he said after a long time, "to weaken what protects her." He waved Despair away. "Go now and return to your post at the orphanage."

Despair bowed and was gone.

"Jealousy," Satan summoned quietly, and a demon appeared before him. "I have a task for you."

Chapter 33

"Hey, Beth, wait up!"

Beth heard someone call her from down the school hallway. She turned and waved. "Hi, Abby."

"Hey," Abby huffed breathlessly, slowing down after rushing to catch up with Beth. "Do you and Becca want to spend the night tonight?" She heaved her backpack strap higher onto her shoulder.

"Umm, sorry, I don't think we can," Beth said. "It's Friday, and my dad wants us to have family night again."

"But that was only while your mom was away, right?" Abby asked. "You mean she's not home yet? It's been, like, a month!"

Beth sighed. She'd been getting this reaction from people a lot lately. "No, she's not home yet. She said that the government doesn't really know what to do with her because we're not from that country and Emma is mentally handicapped."

Abby pouted. "You haven't been able to come over for a long time, Beth. Besides, why are your parents going through so much trouble for a retarded kid?"

Beth stopped walking and turned to face Abby. "I don't know why, okay?" she snapped. "But it's none of your business, so you'll just have to wait for us to sleep over some other time!"

"Well, you don't need to get all mad about it; I was just asking. It doesn't make sense to me, okay? You don't need to freak out."

Beth felt her heart burn with anger. "It doesn't make sense to me either, Abby. But you don't need to be so upset for yourself. I'm the one who doesn't have a mom right now!"

"Okay, okay, sorry," Abby mumbled as she turned and hurried away.

Beth continued toward her classroom, trying not to let the tears spill over. Her mom's voice echoed in her mind: "We've got a new lawyer and he seems much more reliable, but he says that it will be at least another three weeks." Beth remembered what her mom had said about Bahar too. Amy had been so excited because the little girl was raising her hands for Amy to pick her up each day when Amy visited the orphanage.

"Why is that so exciting?" Jealousy whispered, "You can do that and more! Aren't you and Becca and Graham good enough for your parents? Why do they want a child who will cause so much trouble in your lives?"

Gulping down the bubble of anger that was rising in her throat, Beth walked into her classroom and plopped into her chair.

Amy closed the door of her hotel room, dropped her purse on the floor, and lay down on the hard mattress. *Lord, I'm drained,* she prayed.

There had been a meeting that morning with her new attorney, Mr. Abas, and the supposed head of foreign relations in Social Services. Mr. Abas had done fairly well, but the head of foreign relations simply repeated the lines that Mrs. Basar used with Amy and Yasmur numerous times before: "We don't know what to do with you. This is a waste of time. We'll talk about it and get back to you, so you can just go home." Another wasted two hours in a long series of meetings that seemed especially designed to frustrate Amy and send her home in tears.

In the afternoon, she had visited Bahar at the orphanage. She

emma's STORY

could still hear the echoes of Bahar's screams when she put Bahar back into her crib. *Lord, I'm drained,* she thought again, *but we can't give up.*

"Give up, give up," Impatience whispered. "This can't be worth it."

Grace countered immediately. "If all you do here, Amy, is just save that little girl, it would be worth it, for your Father rejoices over one child being found. But you are doing so much more here than just rescuing Bahar. You are the Lord's ambassador in this frightened land."

"No, you aren't," chided Impatience. "Think of how your own children are hurting. Their friends are making fun of them. 'Mom left us for a retarded child'—that's what they're thinking."

The two celestials eyed each other darkly.

Amy threw her pillow across the room. She had been gone for almost two months now without any noticeable progress. Why was she wasting her time? Why was she missing her children and husband over a child she wasn't even sure she could adopt? Yet as soon as she even thought about leaving, Bahar's cries echoed again and the faces of the children at the orphanage appeared in her mind. She was filled with an overwhelming sense of purpose. "All right, Lord, I'm here to stay," she said out loud.

Her cell phone rang, and when Amy picked it up, she heard Mark's voice. "Hey, honey, there's something I need to tell you. It's about your mom."

Chapter 34

Graham, Beth, and Becca piled into their dad's van.

"Beth, can you put my book bag in the back?" Graham asked, passing it over the front seat to where the girls had settled in.

"You just wanted to sit up front, didn't you?" Beth said, taking his bag and shoving it over the back of their seat.

Mark intervened before Graham could respond to Beth's accusation. "No arguing, please. Beth, you could've found a better way to say that; Graham, do I even need to tell you what you should've done?"

"No sir," Graham responded.

The car was silent for a few minutes as Mark maneuvered out of the school parking lot and into traffic.

"Is Grandma going to be hooked up to all those machines again?" Becca asked suddenly.

Mark drove a little further before he answered. "I don't know, Becca. When I visited her last night, she was still hooked up to a few—but not as many as last time. Your grandpa said things weren't as bad this time, so hopefully she'll be home soon."

"What did Mom say last night?" Graham asked, looking at his dad.

"She was pretty upset. She wishes she could be here."

"Then why doesn't she just come home?" Beth blurted.

In the silence that followed, Becca and Graham both stared at their sister, then stared with her at their dad, all three waiting expectantly for his answer. The entire rest of the trip to the hospital, they waited for him to answer, but Mark seemed to be concentrating on the road until they arrived at the hospital.

Becca walked alongside Beth toward Becky's hospital room. "Why did you ask that?" she whispered accusingly.

Beth shot her an angry glance. "Haven't you wondered the same thing?"

Becca shrugged.

"You have!" Beth whispered back, "If Mom wants to come back, why doesn't she? I mean, we tried to adopt Emma, but if it isn't working, maybe it's not God's will."

"Grandma said that our job was to keep going through every door until they all shut," Becca insisted. "We haven't tried every door yet."

"Grandma might die here, Becca; I don't think God would want Mom to be away from her mom when she dies." The look on Becca's face made Beth regret what she had just said.

Becca stopped walking, letting the rest of the family get ahead of them. "How can you say that?" she hissed.

Beth's eyes began to burn with tears. "I'm sorry," she whispered. "I just miss Mom."

Nodding silently, Becca wiped her hand over her own eyes. The girls hurried to catch up with their dad and brother.

"Thank you for picking me up, Ahmed." Amy climbed wearily into the van Ahmed had pulled up in front of the orphanage to take her back to the hotel. She felt as though her energy was sinking along with the sun as it painted the horizon.

"Amy, you look—how do you say it?—beat. You wish you could just take her and go home?"

Amy leaned her head against the window and watched the ever-darkening landscape flash by. "I know that we're doing all we can," she said, "and we're obeying God, so it's good." Then, "I wish I could see my mother."

Ahmed nodded. "Yasmur tells me of her sickness. Becky is a wonderful woman, and it's sad that she is sick. But like you say, Becky and you are to obey God, so it's good."

"Are you a believer, Ahmed?"

"What you and your family do speaks much to me. But it is hard for a Muslim to become a believer, Amy. If I believed, my brother, wife, and children, my whole family would forsake me." He sighed. "It is a serious choice."

Amy nodded, understanding. She knew of many Muslims who had become Christians and been rejected by their families and friends. "You're right, Ahmed. It is a serious choice."

Presently, the van pulled up to Amy's hotel. Ahmed suddenly said, "Amy, would you like to come to dinner with my family tonight? My son is home, and we will have a big meal. You will be much welcome."

Amy looked at the hotel, then back at Ahmed. "I don't know, Ahmed. I'm tired and I have a busy day tomorrow . . ."

Ahmed shook his head and insisted, "Please, I will wait for you here. You must come and be a part of a family this evening."

"Lord, the demon Suffering broke through our defenses," Courage said, "We couldn't stop him before he got to Becky." On God's face, Courage saw a confident compassion that he could never fully understand.

"Yes, I know," the Lord said. "I knew what he would do. And for my name's sake, the fallen one needed to succeed in that task."

Courage drank in the words; the Almighty didn't often tell the angels why he allowed things to happen.

"Satan has planted a seed among Amy's children that we cannot allow to grow," the Lord's wise yet dangerous voice continued. "Jealousy is poisoning hearts and causing needless hurt, and the only way to heal those hearts was to bring them together for an unselfish purpose—through Becky."

Courage looked into the Lord's face. "Lord, Your ways are perfect."

The Lord nodded. "And soon Graham, Beth, and Becca will know that. Now be ready, for I will soon send you to defeat the one who torments Becky."

Chapter 35

"Hello, kids," Becky said with a weak smile as Mark and the children filed into her hospital room.

Tubes and wires laced the bed and the area around Becky, and a heart monitor quietly beeped in a corner. Becca, Beth, and Graham tried to smile back at their grandmother as they formed a tighter circle around their dad. Becca grasped her dad's hand.

"You really should stay only for a few minutes, Mr. Sneed," a nurse said.

Mark nodded and squeezed Becca's hand. "Aren't you kids going to say hi to Grandma?" he asked.

Graham exchanged glances with Mark, then took a deep breath and walked to the side of Becky's bed. Becky turned her head to the side to look at him, "Hey, Graham," she said, a little stronger this time.

"Hi, Grandma. How are you?"

Becky smiled. "Well, I wouldn't say I am hunky dory right now, but I feel better now that I see you."

"We made you some cards," Graham said, handing them to her.

"Oh, thanks, kids," Becky said. "How's your mom?" After an uncomfortable silence, she looked at Mark.

"She's doing well," he replied. "At least, as well as she can be. Yesterday she thought something might be coming up that would get Emma out, but it fell through. She misses you and said that she's praying for you."

Nodding, Becky closed her eyes.

"We miss Mom," Beth blurted.

Becky opened her eyes and looked at her granddaughter. "We all do, sweetie."

"Why is God keeping her away from us and away from you? Doesn't he want her here with you?"

"I don't know why God is doing what he's doing, Beth, or exactly what he wants. But I think you need to talk to your dad about this."

"Mr. Sneed?" A nurse appeared at the door. "It's time."

"We'll see you soon, Mom," Mark said.

That evening at home, Mark called Beth to come talk with him in her bedroom. "So, you're having a hard time with Mom gone," he said.

"Yes, sir," she answered, looking at the carpet. *He's so mad at me,* she thought.

Lord, what in the world am I supposed to do? Mark prayed. *Talks like this were supposed to be Amy's job. Please show me what to do in order to help my daughter the way she needs to be helped.* "Well, Beth—"

"Dad, I'm so sorry!" Beth suddenly exclaimed.

Closing his mouth, Mark let her continue.

Beth felt anger burning up inside her and fought it down, looking back at the carpet. "I'm sorry that I've been so selfish and mean to everyone," she said. "I shouldn't have asked so many questions and made Grandma upset today."

"I forgive you, Beth," Mark said. "It's all right that you have questions and are upset."

Beth looked up in surprise.

"Now, I don't know exactly what's bothering you," Mark said slowly. "But whenever Mom is upset, she usually just likes to tell me everything that's been going on inside her, and we work from there. Would you like to do that?"

Beth felt relief rush through her like a spring breeze. She plopped down in the chair next to her dad and began to talk. "I was excited about having a new sister at first, Dad, and I thought it was cool that we were adopting one of the kids at the orphanage. I was a little scared when Mom first left, because I know Christians aren't always safe over there. But now, I just miss Mom. And I'm scared when I hear about the lawyers and Social Services and how sick Emma is." Eventually, she asked the question that had been bothering her since she had first heard they were going to try to adopt Emma. "Dad, why are we adopting a kid that's mentally handicapped?"

Mark smiled. "That's a great question. I've wondered that a lot too. I suppose you could say that when we first met Emma, your mother and I knew that we were supposed to adopt her. The Holy Spirit tells us things that might seem crazy at first, but usually, when you stop to think about them, they make sense. Beth, do you know that God makes everyone special and with a specific purpose in mind?"

Beth nodded.

"So who's to say that handicapped people are any different? God made Emma and chose to put her in our lives for a specific purpose. Just imagine what that purpose might be."

Beth thought awhile. She thought of her mom being away and what she and her family had been through. She thought of the ways she was beginning to react to people's questions and comments about what her parents were doing. "Well," she began, "I'm more patient with people, especially the ones who think we're crazy to try to adopt Emma."

Mark nodded and smiled. "I know exactly what you mean."

"And now I think differently about handicapped people," Beth continued. "I used to think they were weird and scary because of the way they looked and sounded. But now that I know that I'll have a sister like that, I'm trying to see them more as normal people."

Mark nodded again. "You're right. I think most people think the way you did, but after holding Emma and being with her, I realized after only a few days that she is normal, just like us, only she can't express herself like we do."

Beth smiled. The fear, anger, and jealousy she had felt before was draining away. She was beginning to see her future sister in new ways.

The next morning when Graham came to the hospital, Becky was sitting up reading a magazine. She looked healthier than she had all week.

"Hey, sweetie; did you hear the good news?"

"I did!" Graham answered, sitting on the chair next to the bed. "I saw the doctor before I came up, and he told me that you're all set to go after they do a couple of tests."

Becky sighed and put down her magazine. "Spoiler," she said. "He knew I wanted to tell you."

"I think he's amazed that you pulled through so quickly this time. He didn't think you'd come home quite so soon."

"But here we are," Becky smiled.

"Thank you, God," Graham added. "Did Mark and the kids stop by yesterday?"

"They did, and they gave me this pile of cards right here." She patted the stack of homemade get-well cards on the bedside table.

"We need to pray for them," Graham said. "I saw them a few nights ago, and everyone seemed really depressed, even Mark."

"Well, I understand why," Becky said. "So many people have been discouraging them, asking Mark if he's sure that adopting Emma is God's will, making comments about whether all of this is really worth it. It's so hard not to get discouraged."

"And apparently the kids get teased at school a lot. One kid named Jason keeps teasing Graham."

"And Beth was visibly upset yesterday."

Graham took his wife's hand and said, "Honey, let's pray."

Courage smiled as he watched husband and wife pray. Who would have thought that they would be used by the Almighty in such creative ways to reveal his glory?

Chapter 36

Amy stumbled out of bed as the alarm clock rang. *Good morning, God,* she thought groggily. In the small mirror suspended over the sink, she looked at the dark circles under her eyes. She remembered firing Mr. Abas the evening before, and Mark's call to tell her about his talk with Beth. She wished she could go home and give all three kids big hugs.

Stretching, Amy yawned. It was time to start another day, but her heart felt heavy.

"Stop despairing, Amy," Faith encouraged her. "God has asked you to be a living sacrifice. Living in this hotel and patiently working for Emma is part of living that sacrifice. It's hard now, but if you keep pursuing it for God's glory, you will see his hand everywhere in the end, and your reward will be great."

Taking a deep breath, Amy walked over to the dresser. She felt a bubble of hope rising inside her. She simply had to trust that God was at work.

C·ʝ

"Okay, Amy," Yasmur said as they paused in front of the office door. "I've heard good things about this lawyer from several people, so hopefully this will be the one. Are you ready to do this again?"

The small reception room inside was shabby but clean. Pale sun poured through the window, and the man behind the reception desk looked up and smiled in welcome.

"We're looking for Mr. Mansur," said Yasmur.

"You are here at the right time, ma'am. Mr. Mansur is just returned from a hearing. Whom may I say is looking for him?"

"My name is Yasmur Halici, and this is Amy Sneed. Amy is in need of a lawyer, and my husband recommended Mr. Mansur."

The man's eyes got big. "Amy Sneed?" he asked. "She is the American woman who is trying to adopt a child, am I right?"

"Y-yes, you are right, sir," Yasmur stammered.

"There is much being said about you, Mrs. Sneed," the man said to Amy. "Mr. Mansur has been following your intriguing story."

Yasmur turned to Amy and translated. "Be careful," she added at the end. "We don't want another lawyer who is just hungry for money from the rich American."

Amy nodded and smiled at the man, who was watching them keenly. "I understand," she said.

"Greetings, greetings," Mr. Mansur stood as they entered his office. "It is so good to meet you, after hearing so much about your endeavor."

Mr. Mansur had a warm, sweet face, but his movements were very precise and deliberate. He motioned for the women to sit in two chairs that had been pulled up to the desk. "Now, how may I help you?" he asked.

Lord, I like him so far, Amy prayed. *What do you think?*

Graham was eating lunch at school with Kevin when he heard Kevin say, "Uh-oh. Warning at three o'clock."

Graham glanced up to his right and saw a streak of bright red hair walking toward him.

emma's STORY

"Hey, guys," Jason said, plopping across the table from Graham. Two other boys who always flanked him sat down too. "What's on the menu today?"

"Nothing for you," Kevin said with a defiant glare.

Jason reached over and grabbed Kevin's sandwich. "*Eeeww*, what is this junk?" he said, holding it up to the kid next to him. "It must be something only losers would eat."

Graham tried not to smile. *Jason's big and mean, but his insults are pretty lame*, he thought. But Kevin shot back, "I guess you'd like it then, huh?"

"What's that supposed to mean?" Jason stood up and threw the crumpled sandwich on the ground.

Kevin stood up too.

Oh, boy, Graham thought, putting his own sandwich down. Jason came over and bothered them almost every day, and Graham was sick of the monotony. "Hey, Kevin, just chill," he said.

Jason turned and grinned at Graham. "Yeah, Kevin," he said. "Can't you see Graham doesn't want to get into a fight? He's afraid his mommy will punish him—oh, wait. Graham doesn't have a mommy, does he?"

Jason's teasing always circled around to this. Graham's naturally cool temperament was heating up.

"How long has she been gone now?" Jason continued. "Is she still chasing after that little retarded kid? That's the lamest story I've ever heard. You know what's really happening? I bet your parents are getting a divorce, and your dad made up that story because he's too scared to tell you that your mom's not coming back."

"Graham, you know that Jason's parents were divorced. He's just trying to spread his own hurt," Justice said.

Now Graham stood up, dropping his sandwich, and looked up at the bully.

"Now is not the time to fight," Justice continued. *"You know that fighting will only make it worse and put more stress on your dad. Be a man, Graham; Jason's bullying isn't worth what fighting him will cost."*

Graham felt like he was going to explode any second. He was sick of all the trouble over his mom. He thought of Beth and Becca getting teased all the time; he thought of how people had told his parents just to give up because no child was worth all this trouble; he remembered hearing someone say that this was all his grandparents' fault— their passion for the orphanage kids had gone too far and now they were forcing Mark and Amy to adopt their favorite orphan.

Graham was tired of Jason calling his parents lunatics almost every day. He looked at Jason's laughing mouth. It would feel so good to punch his teeth in right now.

Chapter 37

"Hello, Ayla. How are you today?" Amy and Yasmur smiled at the receptionist in Social Services and chose their seats.

"I am well, thank you, Yasmur." She glanced down the hallway and lowered her voice. "I heard that you and Amy found another lawyer. Is he a good one?"

"We think so. Someone from our church highly recommended him, and we've been impressed with him so far. But we'll see."

"Mrs. Basar will not be pleased, but I hope that you get the little girl soon."

"Thank you," Amy said after Yasmur translated for her. "You are very kind."

Presently, Mr. Mansur appeared. "All right, are you ready?" he asked. He led the way behind Ayla down the hall toward Mrs. Basar's office.

Here we go again, Amy thought. *Lord, please direct Mr. Mansur in a way that will give you the most glory.*

⌘

"So, son, did you hit him?" Mark asked Graham that evening, sitting with him in Graham's room.

"Nah. One of the teachers on lunch duty came up and asked if there was a problem, so Jason and the other guys left." He looked up at Mark. "But Dad, if she hadn't come over, I probably would've punched him."

Mark nodded. "I know how you feel, son, but hitting him would have only made the situation worse."

Graham shrugged and looked down at the comforter on his bed.

"I know how you feel because a lot of adults that your mom and I know have been acting the same way Jason is. They keep telling me that adopting Emma isn't worth it, that we'll probably never be able to do it; that we probably feel pressured into it because Grandpa and Grandma have done so much with Least of These." Mark tried to smile. "The only difference between the adults and Jason is that the adults are trying to be nice about it. But I still get discouraged."

Looking up at his dad, Graham thought he saw tears in his eyes.

That evening, Amy went to a party with Ahmed's family and found herself seated at a table with Ahmed's wife and ten other women, all of whom had heard about Bahar.

"How soon you will be able to adopt her?" one of the women asked in English.

"I don't know. We just had another meeting today with our new lawyer and Social Services. I think it went well, but I don't know."

Another woman spoke up in Turkish, and the first woman translated for the group. "She says that she is a . . . I don't know the word . . . she gives food at parties . . ."

"A caterer? She helps with the food?" Amy asked.

"I think that's right. She says that she was at her job—at a party—and some of the government people . . ."

"Politicians?"

"Yes, that's right! The politicians talked about you. They thought that you should be able to adopt the little girl."

Amy had no idea that her story had spread so far. "That's a surprise!" she said. "I am glad to know this."

"Perhaps they will put good words in for you. Politicians have much power here."

"All right, is everyone ready?" Becky said as she looked at the kids in Graham's class, sitting at their desks. She caught Graham's eye and winked. *Here goes. Lord, all for you,* she prayed. "Mrs. Marshall, will you please turn off the lights?"

Becky heard a big kid in the back of the classroom yawn loudly. Before the lights dimmed, she saw a flash of red hair and knew the kid must be Jason. She nodded to Graham, sitting with a laptop, and a picture of the orphanage appeared on the screen at the front of the room. "Four years ago," she began, "my husband and I visited an orphanage . . ."

Using pictures that they had taken over the years, Becky told the story of Least of These and how she, Graham, Mark, and Amy had met Bahar. As she described the way that the orphans were treated and showed pictures of what the children looked like when she and Graham first arrived at the orphanage, she saw the students' eyes grow bigger and bigger.

Pictures of Bahar finally appeared on the screen. The students saw the first time Amy held her and tried to feed her oatmeal. They watched as, with every trip, Bahar grew thinner and more listless. Becky told them Bahar's story—how her mom had mental problems, how her father killed her mother, how her grandparents died in the earthquake and Bahar was trapped underneath the rubble for three days.

Compassion and Justice watched as the Lord softened the children's hearts and spoke to each of them in a special way, gently rebuking those who had persecuted Graham and his sisters.

"And right now, my son Adam is over there, helping Amy," Becky continued.

When she finished, all the students had tears in their eyes, even Jason.

Chapter 38

"Come on, Emma, just try to eat this," Amy said gently as she coaxed the spoon into Bahar's mouth. But Bahar didn't even try to swallow, and when Amy pulled the spoon out from between her lips, yogurt dripped out of the corner of Bahar's mouth.

"Come on, sweetie," Amy pleaded. "You have to eat. You have to stay strong for when you come home."

She looked helplessly at Adam, who was carrying children out of the Hope Room and putting them into their cribs in the room across the hall. Coming back into the Hope Room, Adam shrugged at Amy, his eyes full of compassion.

Bahar twitched her arms toward Amy. Sighing, Amy put down the bowl of yogurt and lifted Bahar into her arms. "This is all you want, isn't it?" she said, rocking her back and forth. She stroked the stiff dirty peaks of her hair. Bahar's hair had gotten dirtier and dirtier the longer it grew, and now it stood up in clumps that left Amy's fingers feeling oily and stiff whenever she stroked it.

"When we get home, keeping you clean is going to be a chore, huh?" Amy whispered to the sleeping child.

Holding Bahar closer, Amy began to pray. *Lord, I don't know what your plan is for this child, or why you put her in our lives, but please use this for your glory . . .*

"She may never make it home," Doubt whispered.
"Don't believe it, Amy," Hope whispered. "You are obeying God."

Amy's prayer trailed into silence. Why *was* she here? Why was she spending all of this time, money, and energy on this child who could die at any time? Today, Mrs. Basar had sent Mr. Mansur a pile of papers for Amy to sign, and why? She had already signed what felt like a million other papers, and still nothing was happening. Everything in Amy cried to return home, even as she rocked Bahar back and forth and watched her peaceful face. Homesickness overwhelmed her. She knew that if a plane appeared at the door of the orphanage, she would be on it, with or without Bahar.

Ahmed arrived to take Amy and Adam back to their hotel.

Amy sniffed and wiped her eyes, "Okay, thanks, Ahmed. I'll be right there."

As if she knew that Amy was leaving, Bahar suddenly jerked awake.

"I have to go, sweetie," Amy whispered.

Bahar gripped the fabric of Amy's shirt. She clung like a monkey and began to cry and scream.

Amy burst into tears. She couldn't do it! She couldn't take this child back to her crib and leave her in the darkness of the orphanage. She fell into a chair and tried to calm down, holding Bahar closely.

Suddenly, Adam was next to her. "Let me." He gently untangled Bahar from Amy's arms and carried her out of the room. Bahar wailed the entire time.

Amy wondered if she could make it to her room after Ahmed dropped Adam and her off at the hotel.

"Come on, Amy. It'll be all right," Adam said, putting his arm around her and walking with her up the stairs.

"Adam, I don't think I can do this anymore," Amy said.

"I know you can't," Adam agreed. "But God can do it through you." He opened the door to Amy's room and gave her a quick hug.

emma's STORY

"Get some sleep, okay, sis? I flew all the way here to see Emma get out of that orphanage, not to give up. I believe in God and in you. Everything will work out." He smiled and disappeared into his room across the hall.

Sighing, Amy walked into her room and collapsed on the bed. Uncontrollable tears streamed down her face. "God!" she cried. "Please release me from this call. I don't even care about getting this kid out right now; I just want to be home with my family!"

"Grace?" the Father called.

"Yes, Lord?" Grace bowed. The radiant anticipation in the air made him shiver.

"It's time."

Chapter 39

"Master, a large party of angels is going to Social Services," Doubt reported. "They were armed and looked more determined than I have seen in a long time. I fear the worst," he added, cringing.

"We must act immediately!" the dark lord spat as his fist pounded the arm of his throne.

"My lord," said Doubt, hesitantly, "if you move quickly, we can stop them before they fulfill your enemy's purpose."

Satan glared and the demon cringed. Nevertheless, Satan began to give out orders. "Jealousy! Despair! Chaos!" he shouted.

The three demons appeared and bowed quickly.

"Doubt has just reported a large group of angels heading to Social Services. This could be our final victory."

"What will you have us do, lord?" Jealousy bowed again.

"I am sending more demons to each of your divisions. Crush whatever angels you see immediately. Chaos, they will attack your division first, so I will send the most demons to you. Keep fighting until you have triumphed!"

"And sign here," Mr. Mansur said, pointing to another line.

Amy wrote her name again, and the last paper went back in a folder with all the rest. "Whew, I think that is the most papers I've ever signed in one sitting!"

"It was a lot," said Mr. Mansur, "but it just might be enough. We have done our best. Now we must go to Social Services and submit the papers."

Their taxi was quickly surrounded by traffic. "Where did all these cars come from?" Amy asked.

"Maybe there is an accident," Mr. Mansur suggested. "But car accidents are so rare here; I have only seen a few myself."

Chaos laughed as he watched the back of the ambulance open up and the medics jump out and rush to two cars smashed like soda cans in the middle of the road.

"This will keep them a little detained, won't it?" He nudged Confusion and pointed to Amy's taxi.

Confusion laughed and turned to the officer who was trying to direct traffic. "Look at all of those cars backed up. Do you even remember how to direct them around an accident? When was the last time this happened while you were on duty?"

The other demons snickered and spread themselves around the scene.

"Demons, stop your tricks." Justice was flanked by six other angels.

"You're too late to stop this mess, angel," Chaos shot back, pulling out his sword. "We're here to stop whatever our master's enemy has planned."

Justice's eyes lit up with a heavenly fire as he and the angels with him drew their swords.

"You can't stop us!" Chaos yelled. "What are you trying to accomplish?"

"You should know my purpose already, demon, for you were once an angel of light who served the Ancient of Days." Justice ducked and tried to hit Chaos in the stomach, but the demon twisted out of the way. All the angels and demons lunged into battle.

Chaos scowled and slashed at Justice, nicking his shoulder. "Spare me from the worship of your master; I've heard enough of it."

"And you'll continue to hear it all of eternity," Justice said, shrugging off his wound. His sword caught Chaos in the neck. The demon winced

and pulled away, dodging Justice's next thrust, but it hit him directly in the chest. Chaos lifted his head and howled.

Amy relaxed a little as the taxi edged forward.

"Looks like we're finally moving," Mr. Mansur said.

"Finally," said Yasmur and Adam together.

The taxi passed the scene of the accident, and thirty minutes later, Amy and the others were sitting in Mrs. Basar's office.

Grace, Faith, Compassion, and a large assembly of angels stood around the room with their backs to the humans, watching for demons.

Amy and Mr. Mansur seated themselves in the two chairs in front of the desk, and Adam and Yasmur stood to one side.

Mrs. Basar had stopped being hospitable two months ago. She nodded curtly. She took the folder that the lawyer handed her and fingered through the papers, sometimes pausing to read a few lines. Presently, she closed the folder. "I am going to be honest with you," she said, looking at Amy.

Wow, thank you, Lord, that's a first! Amy prayed.

"You have been here for three months now, and you have worked tirelessly to adopt this child. I and the rest of Social Services have decided that you are an adequate candidate for adoption, and that it is in the child's best interest to be adopted by you and your husband." From the top of her desk she picked up what looked like a certificate.

Amy gripped the sides of her chair and tried to breathe.

"Yasmur," said Adam, "did she mean what she said? Does this mean that Emma is Amy's now?"

Yasmur opened her mouth but no words came out.

Mr. Mansur held out his hand and took the final piece of paper. He quickly signed his name, then put the pen in Amy's hand and pointed to where she was to sign. Then he took the pen from her and said in English, "Congratulations, Mrs. Sneed. It is finished."

Chapter 40

A my grinned. "So that's it? Well, what are we waiting for?"
She shook Mrs. Basar's hand, thanking her in Turkish;
then, holding the certificate like a trophy, she marched out of the
office triumphantly, followed by Adam, Yasmur, and Mr. Mansur.

"Ayla, look!" she squealed.

When Ayla saw the certificate, she began to shout in Turkish.
Amy couldn't understand anything Ayla said, but the two women
hugged and shouted happily together. Office doors opened and
workers came out into the hallway and smiled. Mrs. Basar stood in
her doorway, hands on her hips and a sour expression on her face.

*"Holy is the Lord!" Grace and his companions cried. "The author
and maker of life!" Suddenly, Grace's voice was broken by a twisted sword
that protruded from his chest. The angel gave a cry of surprise and fell
to his knees while his companions scattered. Yelling hideously, a crowd of
demons appeared and attacked the angels.*

"Stop Amy!" Chaos cried, pointing to her.

*Whipping out his sword, Faith continued the angels' song, only this
time, he shouted it, "Holy, holy is the King! Holy, holy is the Author!"*

*Rallying around the group of humans, the angels formed an
unbreakable mass. They began to hack through the demon hordes pouring
at them.*

*"We outnumber them ten to one!" Chaos roared over the sound of
the battle. "Crush them and get to Amy!"*

*The angels tightened their circle, all shouting Faith's battle cry in
powerful unison. Compassion cried out as Prejudice wounded him.*

emma's STORY

As the demons pressed in from all sides, more and more angels slumped over. Small holes began to appear in the protective circle.

"Amy!" Yasmur suddenly exclaimed, pointing to her watch. "It's almost four o'clock! That's less than an hour to get to the orphanage before it closes for the weekend."

"Let's go!" Adam cried.

Mr. Mansur put a foot on the street and waved his hand for a taxi. He had to leap back onto the sidewalk as it raced by. "It almost killed me!" he exclaimed.

"Here's another one." Adam stayed on the sidewalk as he waved at the driver. But the driver didn't seem to see them and the taxi rushed by.

Shame snickered as he watched the scene from inside the taxi. "You'll never get one today, Amy," he spat.

"Four fifteen," Yasmur announced. "It's never been this hard to get a taxi. This is ridiculous. We're not going to make it now. They try to close early on Fridays."

"Come on, Yasmur, be optimistic," Adam said, looking down the road for another taxi. *God, please, I want to see Emma before I leave on Sunday. But have your way.* Another taxi pulled onto the road and approached the curb where the foursome stood.

"The fool," Chaos smirked to himself when he saw Adam's hopeful gaze. He whispered to the taxi driver, "Go faster, there's no one there." The driver pushed the accelerator.

"That's enough, Chaos," Justice grasped the demon's arm and whirled him around.

"Here we go," Adam called as the taxi pulled up to the curb. "Everyone hop in."

◌◌

Sighing, Beth pushed herself higher up in her chair and folded her arms across her desk. Her teacher had given them another twenty minutes to do their homework, but Beth had already turned hers in. She pulled out a piece of paper and began to draw.

Beth, it's time to pray.

Beth scrawled MOM on the bottom of her paper. What was her mom doing now? When Adam had left for Turkey, he was hoping to see Bahar released. Beth knew better than to get too hopeful.

Beth, it's time to pray.

Beth looked around. *God, are you telling me to pray?* She bowed her head and began, *God, please help my mom and Adam right now. I pray that whatever's happening right now will glorify you.*

◌◌

"Four forty-five," Yasmur announced.

"What is with all of this traffic?" Adam tapped the dashboard impatiently with his fingers as the driver shouted at the other cars on the road.

"Adam, take it easy. I'm impatient too," Amy said quietly. Brother and sister exchanged glances; then both began to pray silently.

As the taxi moved, so did the angelic battle around them.

The ride seemed to take two hours. The air in the taxi was tight and tense. Amy's prayer gave in to her impatience. "Hurry up! Hurry up!" she urged the driver.

The taxi finally pulled up to the orphanage. "Let's go!" Adam shouted.

They heard shouting behind them as they ran toward the handicapped building.

"Oops!" Yasmur said. "We forgot to pay the driver."

"You go on. I'll get it," Mr. Mansur called.

Dodging the holes in the sidewalk, Amy, Adam and Yasmur ran toward the handicapped building. "We have to make it," Amy cried. "What time is it?"

"Five o'clock!" Yasmur exclaimed. "Maybe they're running late too."

Despair snickered.

Adam pushed on the door and shook the handle. It was locked. "Let us in!" Amy called.

"Hey, we need to get in!" Adam shouted, banging on the door. "Have they ever opened the door after closing time?" he asked Yasmur.

"I don't think so."

Anger, Doubt, and Suffering braced themselves against the door, grunting.

"Just go back, it's too late," Despair hissed to Amy. "You can come back on Monday."

"Please, God, don't let this stop us," Amy said out loud, hitting the door again. "Emma! Emma! Can you hear me? We've come to get you!"

Amy leaned against the building and whispered, "Lord, don't let this be the end. Bahar might not make it another weekend." Then her legs folded under her, and she began to cry.

"Just give up, angels," Despair spat, circling Hope and Strength as they stood protectively over Bahar. *"It's too late. You know Bahar won't live through the weekend, and the humans have missed their chance to save her."*

"Your lies are meaningless." Hope swung his sword hungrily. *"You will not win this battle."*

"You see how weak she is," Despair continued. *"She's suffering so much. Just let me end it."*

Strength gave a cry and lunged toward the demon. *"Your master will not get the glory from this girl!"*

emma's STORY

Chapter 41

A *sudden blast of heavenly light threw every demon to the ground in the handicapped building. They screeched; covering their eyes and ears and curling up in terror. The room was transformed with the presence of the Holy Spirit. Even the angels were filled with a kind of dread, and they fell to their knees in awe and reverent delight.*

"Have you come to torment us before our time?" Despair screeched.

Strength and Hope smiled. "Holy, holy," they whispered.

The Father's voice echoed through the rooms. "I will have that which proclaims my glory."

Suddenly, the door opened.

"Amy!" Adam shouted. "It's open. Come on!"

A fresh surge of strength rushed through Amy, and she scrambled to her feet and followed Adam into the reception room of the handicapped building. "Here it is," Amy said, handing the paper to Delar, who was putting her coat on, preparing to leave. Amy absently wondered why the woman hadn't opened the door for them, but she was too excited to dwell on it.

Delar's eyes got big as she read the paper. Rapidly, Yasmur began to explain what was going on. Delar took her coat off, sat down at the reception desk and studied the certificate, glancing from Yasmur, to Amy, then back to the certificate. Eventually conceding to the document's authenticity, Delar shouted something down the hallway. A group of the workers appeared and crowded around.

"Is this true?" Fatima's voice called down the hallway. When she appeared, she saw the paper and the looks on the workers' faces. "It *is* true!" she shouted, throwing her arms around Amy and Adam.

"It is! It is!" Amy cried.

"Derya! Emma is going home!" Fatima called.

"What?" Derya appeared at the doorway, coat in hand.

"Emma's going home with Amy!"

Derya shouted triumphantly and began to jump up and down.

Mr. Mansur pushed himself through the crowd. "Mrs. Sneed," he said, "the taxi is waiting for you. Here, let me finish this." He grabbed the certificate from Delar and said something that spurred her to action. She spoke rapidly to the workers. One of them disappeared down the hall and reappeared with Bahar in her arms.

When the little girl saw Amy, she stretched her arms out to her.

"Emma, Emma," Amy whispered as she took her. "You're mine now, sweetie. It's over." All of the pressure of the last three months melted off Amy. It was time to go home.

After quick, tearful good-byes to Fatima and Derya, the group left the handicapped building. Amy held Bahar as if she would never let her go.

The trees around them danced and waved as the Father blew a soft breeze through them.

"Look, Amy," Adam said. "Even the trees are celebrating this day."

The demons cowered before their lord's throne, tense and anxious in the icy silence. None of the demons looked at each other, and no one spoke. Each was poised, waiting in pain for their dark lord to move or speak.

Satan gazed blankly at his minions, these dark servants who had failed him. He clutched the arms of his throne so tightly that his clawed, skeletal hands began to pop and crack.

He had lost.

When God called his angels together, his smile made the air shimmer and shiver with excitement. Countless celestials bowed before him, exulting in his presence and waiting anxiously for him to speak.

"Arise, angels," he said. "You have done well. You have fought and not grown weary and have obeyed my every command."

He turned to Hope and Strength, who bowed again. "You have waited patiently for my timing and defeated legions of demons."

"You have overseen and accomplished numerous tasks." This time Grace bowed.

"You have fought for my truth and administered my healing." Reverently, Justice and Courage bent their heads.

"You have encouraged and commanded." Unity, Compassion, and Faith bowed.

"And through it all, you have sung my praise and trusted in my wisdom, even when you did not know what I was doing. You have brought glory to my name through this story.

"A country wrapped in darkness has been opened to my light, and Satan's reign continues to break. Emma's story will continue, and she will be used by me and will grow stronger in the care of Mark and Amy and their family. All who see her will know that she has been marked for a special purpose. I will fulfill my work through my precious Emma."

Excitement and anticipation rippled through the army before him.

"Although this country has been shown my glory, there is still much to reveal to them. They must learn more of my love and grow in me. And *this is only one of many countries that have not heard my name. I will take more of my children, like Graham and Becky, Mark and Amy, on journeys to reveal my glory where the darkness still hides it. My love will pour down on all peoples.*

"But this story is not over." The Lord turned to a different angel. "Providence."

The angel bowed. "Yes, Lord?"

"There is a sixteen-year-old girl in Virginia whom I have chosen to play a part in revealing my glory through Emma's story. She has a dream to write a book before she graduates. I am going to fulfill that dream. Graham and Becky have friends who are leading a Bible study for teenagers at her church. Make sure she goes to that Bible study. Through these friends, she will learn of this adoption and write a book about Emma that I will use to touch nations."

Providence bowed and was gone.

The Father's eyes were full of love, excitement, and passion. As he finished speaking, he sat back, and the angels began to worship.

The pale morning sun filtered through the hotel window and across Emma's face. Squeezing her eyes shut, she rolled over and ran her fingers over the fabric of the comforter. A bird outside the window began to sing joyfully, bringing Emma into full wakefulness.

She sniffed; the air was different. She rolled her fingers back over the comforter. It was soft and warm. There was no bare fluorescent bulb flickering above her head, suspended from a cracked and splotchy ceiling. Her hair felt clean around her face. Where was she?

Confused, Emma rolled over and saw Amy lying next to her in the bed, watching her. Oh! For several moments, Emma gazed

emma's STORY

deeply into Amy's eyes. Finally, Amy reached up and touched her finger to Emma's nose and whispered, "Good morning, Emma Ruth Sneed."

Emma's dark eyes looked at Amy solemnly, and then her mouth parted into a peaceful smile.

The Father smiled too.

Epilogue

When we first met Bahar in the fall of 1999, she had just come to the orphanage after having witnessed her father kill her mother and after being trapped under a building for three days following a horrific earthquake. At that point she still had pierced ears and curly black hair. By the time that we were able to free her from the clutches of evil, her head had been shaved and she weighed only twenty-five pounds; she had kidney stones; her teeth were overtaken by forty cavities, and mentally she was completely withdrawn into her own little world.

It wasn't until 2002 that the laws in Turkey passed that would allow us to adopt Bahar. Amy traveled to Turkey and spent three months dealing with the Turkish bureaucracy to try to get Bahar free. Hour after hour, day after day, she and Bahar held on to the hope that God would make a way.

Five years later, the Bahar we knew in the dark world of the orphanage is gone, though not forgotten. The sick, tired, scared Bahar has been replaced by a joyous, happy, and full-of-life Emma!

Emma has gone through evaluation after evaluation and test after test to help us figure out how to make her quality of life better. We started by "peeling away the layers" of what had happened to her over the years—fixing what we could and learning to live with what we couldn't.

The first objective was to get her basic nutritional needs met. Emma underwent intensive dental treatment so that she could begin to eat. We then got her on high doses of vitamins and nutritional supplements to get her weight up, get her hydrated, and start to build up her basic nutritional structure. The next step was to see what could be done with physical therapy and braces for her legs. At the same time, it was also determined that she was having visual problems, so we had a surgery done to correct that problem.

From there we started getting help to figure out what was going on inside her mind. Numerous brain scans, MRIs, and other tests were done. The results of these tests at times were disheartening, to say the least. Emma was diagnosed by the professionals with having many different types of brain disorders; some even said that she would not live more than a couple of more years.

We quickly realized that diagnoses in the medical world often depend more on opinions and the personalities of the professionals than hard facts. We have learned to choose professionals who admit that they don't have all of the answers but are willing to take the time to look at Emma as an individual rather than a number on a chart. God has brought those types of professionals into our lives more often than not.

Most recently, Emma was evaluated by several doctors from a special organization. They determined that Emma's hip was dislocated and that she needed to have a surgery to correct this problem or she would spend her life in pain. As of the writing of this epilogue, Emma has just had the surgery, and she is wearing an almost full-body cast for ten weeks. The surgeon was pleased that the surgery was not as invasive as they had first feared, and she is hopeful about a quick recovery. She also has said that this surgery could very well make it possible for Emma to learn to walk!

Mentally, Emma has made great strides. She has come from not saying anything and being very withdrawn to being an outgoing, happy, and loving little girl. Her vocabulary includes about twenty words, but she communicates in her own way and she understands more than we give her credit for.

We have found a wonderful school for Emma, where she is in kindergarten with other children and where she has learned many things over the past couple of years. The other children have taken to her and have accepted her for who she is. Her school has children from kindergarten through twelfth grade, and Emma is known and loved by all of them. She and her pink wheelchair cause even the toughest high school boy to stop and give her a hug or to say a kind word! We saw evidence of this during her recent surgery when every one of the kids in the school wrote her a letter of encouragement. We are very blessed to have a school that cares for Emma and that knows she is a child of God!

Touching lives is not just limited to her school friends. Everywhere we go, people take notice of Emma and want to hear her story. We have had the opportunity to tell her story to people in the grocery store, to the doctors who have examined her, to workers that come to our house, and to business associates, neighbors, and numerous others who have come into our lives. Telling Emma's story has allowed us to share how God loves each and every one of us and how he has a plan for all our lives—even the "least of these." Those who hear Emma's story will tell us that she is a very lucky girl, or that she is blessed to have us in her life—our reply is always to say that we are the ones who are blessed by having her in our lives!

In the five years that Emma has been a part of our family she has made great strides, but she still has a long way to go. We are hopeful that through love, prayer, and attention to her physical needs, Emma will continue to improve. She may not become president or win a Nobel Prize for physics, but God's love will continue to be reflected through her.

Most children start laughing and enjoying life within months of being born. For Emma it has taken eight years, but she has now finally found her laugh, and we look forward to seeing how her laugh and life affect those with whom she comes in contact.

God is truly an awesome God, and we hope that you see through this book that he can use anyone for his glory. Remember that no matter what obstacles you face in life, God *can* make a way!

—Mark and Amy Sneed
parents of Emma Ruth Sneed

Least of These Ministries is based out of Arizona and is dedicated to sending "Hug Teams" to minister to orphans around the world. If you can hug a child, you can be used greatly by God to reveal His glory.

To find out more about Hug Teams and Least of These Ministries, please go to www.LoTMinistries.org.